It Never Pays To Laugh Too Much

Gertrude Story

It Never Pays To Laugh Too Much

THISTLEDOWN PRESS

Canadian Cataloguing in Publication Data

Story, Gertrude, 1929 -
    It Never Pays To Laugh Too Much

ISBN 0-920066-86-0 (bound).
ISBN 0-920066-87-9 (pbk.)

I. Title.
PS8587.T67I8 1984   C813'.54   C84-091137-8
PR9199.3.S86I8 1984

50,604

All the characters in this book are fictitious and any resemblance to actual persons living or dead is coincidental.

Book design by A.M. Forrie
Cover painting by Marie Elyse St. George

Typesetting by Résistance Graphics, Edmonton
Set in 12 point Plantin

Printed and bound in Canada by
Hignell Printing Limited, Winnipeg

Thistledown Press
668 East Place
Saskatoon, Saskatchewan
S7J 2Z5

For Joseph Le Roy Story, who knows now all there is to know.

For St. Gertrude, who knows this traveler well.

And for Lelttitia, who now demands I strive to know her best.

Acknowledgements:

The author wishes to thank the Saskatchewan Arts Board and the Banff Centre School of Fine Arts for their financial assistance which aided her in the completion of this book.

These stories have been published previously:
"At A Party It Never Pays To Laugh Too Much" — *Newest Review*, "Car of Maroon" — *Canadian Author and Bookman*, "But First You Ought To Ask The Bride" — *Canadian Ethnic Studies*, "One Time In Winter" — *Newest Review*, "The Summer Visitor" — *Saskatchewan Gold*, and "Never Be A-Scared To Dance" — *Camrose Review*.

"But First You Ought To Ask The Bride" has been an award winner in the CBC Literary Competition and subsequently broadcast on CBC "Anthology".

"How Come A Angel Could Ever Be Called A Swan?" has been broadcast on CBC "Ambiance".

This book has been published with the assistance of the Saskatchewan Arts Board and The Canada Council.

*Against pain
my only shield
is calculated
laughter.*

CONTENTS

My Grampa Schroeder would not be called Opa. He was too modern; you had to call him Grampa, and that was that. My Oma Schroeder would not be called Grandma. She said that it was awful; it was English, and so it wasn't right.

At our house, Mama said on her side of the family there wasn't such a commotion heard about. At our house, Mama said Grampa Schroeder was stubborn; stubborn ran pretty strong in the Schroeders. Grampa Schroeder was too proud, she said; what was wrong, she'd like to know, with the word Opa? It was a good word; he'd pay yet, for letting go of the old ways. And not to go to church, why, he'd wind up in hell yet and who would be able to stop it? Didn't Papa ever worry about that?

At my Cousin Gerda's house, Auntie Elizabeth said it was Oma was stubborn. Oma was trapped in old country ways, she said, and Auntie Elizabeth was sorry for her. At my Cousin Gerda's house, Auntie Elizabeth called Oma Schroeder Mother; or she called her Grandmother, if it was in front of Gerda and Murray and Floydie. In front of Elsa, too, of course, before Elsa went and let herself into the stallion. And after she got called Grandmother once too often at my Cousin Gerda's house, Oma Schroeder never went there any more.

Grampa Schroeder never went to church, and it seemed to worry Mama. Oma Schroeder went to church, though, and Auntie Elizabeth used to. When she lived at Grampa Schroeder's-Oma Schroeder's, boy, Auntie Elizabeth used to. Until you got married, if you lived at Oma Schroeder's house you went to church or she quit cooking for you. But she couldn't quit cooking for Grampa Schroeder. In Germans that wasn't allowed.

Grampa and Oma's family ran strong to boys. First there was Papa and Uncle Abe, and then there was Auntie Elizabeth. And Papa and Uncle Abe were good, — no trouble. And they minded their own business good, too. Auntie Elizabeth was bright. She was bright, so bright, Grampa Schroeder once wanted to make her a teacher.

So first there was Papa and Uncle Abe and Auntie Elizabeth. Then after a while, after a few years, there came Uncle Emil. Not Gerda's papa. Gerda's papa was Uncle Emil Beckmann. So I had two Uncle Emils and I even had two Cousin Emils, too. If Germans like a name, boy, almost everybody gets named it. And no family cares if there's a Emil in every house in the country. On both Mama's and Papa's side we ran strong to Abes and Emils and Emmas.

Not Alberts, though. There was only one Albert. That was Papa. Not Elizabeths, either. Only Papa's side had an Elizabeth: that was Cousin Gerda's mama. And once I heard Mama tell my Aunt Emma — the Aunt Emma on *her* side, — that one Elizabeth was quite enough and plenty.

Auntie Elizabeth was bright. On Papa and Auntie Elizabeth's side, it was a good thing to be bright: Grampa Schroeder really liked it.

Good was another thing. To be good was another good thing. But then along came Uncle Emil — bright — who, right from a baby started out not liking Uncle Abe — not so bright — and never ever changed his mind about it, either, even though Uncle Abe all his life was good and nice and smiley, and good, too, at minding his own business.

Emils seemed to be hard to bring up; Oma Schroeder once said so. And Auntie Elizabeth, who nearly got to be a teacher, changed diapers for one Emil and then, next thing, she went and married another one. So she wound up with two doses of Emils.

Auntie Elizabeth could talk sparkly. If you once got her talking, and if there was only women around, she could talk real sparkly. More than Mama, even, though Auntie Elizabeth didn't get to be a teacher and Mama did.

People not liking other people is a funny thing. To start as young as Uncle Abe and Uncle Emil did, seems to me a funny thing. Somehow it seems that not liking somebody has to do with things that the not-likers don't even know about; or maybe nobody really knows about. So with Uncle Abe and Uncle Emil, I think everybody scolded about it a lot, but nobody ever tried to find out why.

And after Uncle Emil came and was bad and bright and always pulled hair and hollered at Uncle Abe, even when Uncle Abe always tried to give him the things he wanted — his cookie or his play train, or just anything Uncle Emil wanted, — then there came Uncle John and Uncle Peter and Uncle Luke. Only they died and were nothing but white marble lambs with peaceful faces and their knees folded up under them, saying they were *SAFE IN THE ARMS OF JESU*, only all in German, in the graveyard.

And then came Aunt Emma. Papa's dancing and laughing Emma. Grampa's bright and sparky Emma. Oma's quiet and good Emma. And then came Uncle Arnie, who was a baby but grew up in lots of time to go away to the war.

And later at Grampa-Oma's place was Laura, too, but she was different. Grampa Schroeder found her in a clothes basket with Auntie Elizabeth, who never finished Normal School but went instead all the way to Toronto one day, telling not a single solitary soul, but with the last two cow creamery cheques Grampa had given her to cash for him in town, in her pocket.

But when he brought her back home again, — went right to Toronto and found her and brought her back home again to finish Normal School — Uncle Emil Beckmann came riding up on his snow white stallion, his stallion with the thick, thick neck and fire in its breathy pink nostrils, his awful big stallion with the rolling wide white eyes.

And the next thing people knew, Auntie Elizabeth belonged to Uncle Emil Beckmann, and he gave her his name and that's about all, so Grampa Schroeder said.

And Auntie Elizabeth never went back to Normal School; she birthed Elsa too quick. And Uncle Emil Beckmann said Laura better stay at Grampa Schroeder's; he didn't say it until after the wedding. And Auntie Elizabeth is supposed to have cried and cried, — cried something wicked — but Laura stayed.

Laura was older. Laura at Grampa-Oma Schroeder's was older than me but I was older than Gerda, only just a little. And Elsa was older than me and she was older than Gerda. Elsa had white, white hair and pink watery eyes, and she was so good she went young one night into Uncle Emil's stallion and got made into a angel, and then she wasn't there anymore.

That's when my Cousin Gerda quit talking. "Funny thing," Mama said, "a funny thing she should do that; I heard they were always scrapping. Cat and dog, they were always scrapping." And Papa said, "Well, I don't know so much about that, there's lots more there than meets the eye."

Then Mama put her mending basket down and took off her spectacles and rubbed her eyes. "The light's poor again," she said. "Do you mean it left her a little bit queer? That little Gerda was always an odd one; too bright for her own good. It doesn't pay in a girl; look at your sister

Elizabeth and tell me it ever pays in a girl."

Papa had got up and lifted down the gas mantle lamp as
soon as ever Mama said the light was poor again. He
screwed out its pump so that it popped up from inside
where the gas and the air was and he started to pump it,
whump, whump, whump. When he talked there was a
whump for maybe every second word.

"I *don't* think she's *queer* at *all*," Papa said, making his
voice loud at the whumps so that she could hear him. "I *tell*
you, I *don't* think she's *queer* at *all*."

"You don't have to get sore," Mama said. "Just because I
wonder if she got left a little bit queer. You don't have to go
and get sore just because it's on *your* side."

"I'm *not* sore," Papa said. But he hung the gas mantle
lamp back up with a jerk that set it swinging. It had no business swinging and making long swinging shadows on
everything all over the floor and ceiling and walls. And
Mama said, "Well if you're not sore, then stop that." And
he did; he reached up and held the lamp in both his hands
to stop it, and then he took his spectacles out of his bib
overall pocket and sat down and then got up again and went
into the parlour.

"Aren't you coming back?" Mama called after him. "Are
you going to sit in there all alone? For a man who is not
sore, you're acting mightly peculiar."

And Papa came back in then, carrying one of the green
encyclopedias — he was up to MOR already, and I wasn't,
yet — and Mama said, "Oh oh, I see; you were just getting
something to read."

But she just hardly let him get started.

"Well maybe not *queer*," she said, "but look what happened at the funeral."

And Papa looked up quick; he was thinking of MOR-
something already, I guess, and Mama sort of surprised
him. And he just jerked his head towards me where I sat on
the big footstool with another encyclopedia — I was only

up to BRA — and the encyclopedia was open, but I guess I'd forgot to turn a page for quite a while, maybe.

And Mama didn't even look my way, she just kept sewing. "They're better off hearing it at home," she said. "They're better hearing it right; at home."

And Papa said, "Enough is enough." And he shut the encyclopedia and went and clappered his pipe out, spewing the mess into the coals of the Quebec heater and making quite a bit of noise. He looked at Mama and just for a minute there, he had these power, power eyes. "Leave the kid alone," he said. "Just leave the kid alone."

"So you *are* sore," Mama said. "You get the least little bit put out over me saying nothing but the truth and right away you look at me with those wild Schroeder eyes and start ranting at me. What did *I* do? I only said that young Gerda has got the Schroeder way to put a stubborn head along with a weak mind and so she's likely gonna be a little bit queer all her life; and that's the facts of it, and all your ranting and defending, just because it happens to be on *your* side, won't change one jot or a tittle, and even if you pray to God for it, it won't."

Papa stood there for all she said. His eyes had the power in them whilst she said it. When she was done he opened his mouth as if to maybe say something, but then just all at once the power left and his eyes got old, somehow, and he walked out to the porch and then next thing we heard the door open and then close again with just a little click; Mama did not like door bangings, didn't I ever know it.

Aunt Emma Uhrich once said, — Mama's own Sister Emma once said — Mama got away with murder because Papa was twelve years older and pure crazy about her. And when Papa went out like that — with only a little click of the door latch, too — I all at once thought to myself that

this kind of killing with words was what Aunt Emma
Uhrich must have meant.

*It is a terror to think of those past things with the crystal
clarity of a child's computer mind. I am not afraid of much; I
am too old for that. But I am still afraid of pain: I have not
the mind to train myself out of it; I have not the heart to let
myself forget.*

*You do not think of them, the ones of your blood: those who
suffered pain, and caused it — all, all of them, misunderstood.
You do not think of them for far too many years, and all at
once they are there, and it is all painful/happy.*

*Our Oma Schroeder was a singer. Nobody else in all the
family, or the world, even, could sing like our Oma Schroeder
sang. In the strawberry patch she sang to God: humm-humm,*
Jesu-treu; *humm, humm, humm. In the barn, milking cows,
she sang whole prayers to God: O give them good health, Lord;
let this milk be my wine. In the strawberry patch her voice was
like a golden bee bumbling honey; in the barn it was like a bell
of yellow brass, rich and full and clear.*

*But in church! Oh, the glory in church, when our Oma
Schroeder opened up her honey throat and answered the
pastor's* **Kyrie eleison, Christe eleison,** *with her own!
Eyes closed, head bowed, she stood, and the music started with
a hum behind her teeth, with her lips almost shut on the* **Kyri-e:**
that was the bee bumbling in the strawberry patch.

Then, **e-lei-ei-son,** *she parted her lips, her full praising
lips, and the prayer started: that was the blessing of the cows.
Then she threw her head back and her full and heavy bosom
rose, and,* **Chri-ste e-l-ei-ei-so-o-o-nn,** *the glory poured out
thick and high, high-pitched, high; through the mouth and nose
and eyes and throat the glory poured and shimmered and rang*

so honey rich and golden, the voices of sixty other singers, even the pastor's, were only the background to her song.

But at Elsa's funeral Oma Schroeder could not sing. She sat beside my Cousin Gerda, who had not spoken a word since they found what was once Elsa on the floor of the stallion's box-stall. Auntie Elizabeth would not come to the church and Floydie wasn't supposed to — he wasn't trained yet. Grampa Schroeder did not come either; he would not be pushed away by Auntie Elizabeth; he was home with her whether she wanted him or not. He said he knew where he belonged.

That left only Oma and Gerda and Uncle Emil to have the family seats beside the coffin, right beside the coffin, so that once in a while their knees touched it. And when all the people were gathered and the family came in, Gerda had that stubborn look and would not sit beside Uncle Emil; she went the other side around and moved her chair — in front of all those people she moved her chair — and put Oma in the middle in the family seats, and sat there looking straight ahead and stubborn. Gerda was good at that.

It is a terror to think of those past things with the crystal clarity of a child's computer mind.

And Uncle Emil sat straight and tall and so beautiful, beautiful, in his black suit and white shirt and black-as-midnight tie; his golden hair and beard as neat and trim and beautiful as the prince of a royal house. He did not cry. He opened the hymn book at the right places. He stood and sat and kneeled and sang and prayed, all in the right places.

But Gerda and Oma Schroeder sat and were still.

And then the pastor spoke. He spoke of Elsa, white and beautiful in the glory of an angel in heaven at God the Father's left hand. She had been a dutiful and a loving daughter to her earthly father, the pastor said, and that dutiful and beauteous spirit had therefore gone to sit as an angel in heaven where she would stay forever and ever, bound to God's heavenly throne.

And that is when Gerda got up from her chair, looking neither to left nor to right, and turned and stepped before Uncle Emil sitting there straight and beautiful and with power still strong in his eyes.

She laughed.

She laughed into his beautiful eyes and she said, "Papa, go and scrape the rest of me from off the stallion's hooves before you ride again to talk brotherhood of man with Mrs. Elmyra Bitner."

Then she laughed again, laughed this clear, clear, clear laugh again, and stepped into her place again, and sat down.

It is a terror to think of things past with the crystal clarity of a child's computer mind.

And the pastor closed his Bible, trying not to seem too fast about it, maybe, and nodded at Mrs. Kneiper at the organ to start to play.

And though I do not want to remember, I remember. The people then, that day, would not or could not sing: not our Oma Schroeder, nor Uncle Emil, nor Papa and Mama; not even the pastor or anybody else in that church. But as she stood there, shining, her head thrown back and her arms stretched out, palms up, in some solitary kind of longing, our Oma's voice poured crystal clear and soaring, **Kyrie, Christe eleison,** *from the flowing fountain of my Cousin Gerda's throat.*

When you had a party to go to at our house, you had to hurry. You had to shine up your shoes good, and no mistake. Nobody went anywhere from out of our house without shining their shoes, and nobody came in for a party to find you with shoes dirty or — shame, shame, worse — with manure on them. It was like Mama had read a rule somewhere once and kept it: If you don't shine your shoes to walk out public in front of people, you're a no-good and people will laugh at you.

People not laughing at you was what ruled Mama and was supposed to rule me too. The trouble was, I *liked* them to laugh. I was a girl, but I liked them to laugh.

In the schoolyard when Otto Schroeder — not the Cousin Schroeders, but the other ones — when Otto Schroeder or my Cousin Abe Schroeder said things smark aleck, the girls were supposed to stand by and giggle; put their hands up over their mouths and look at each other eyes-wide, and giggle. Only *I* sometimes told them things smart aleck right back, and they sometimes laughed and said I was a corker, but mostly they didn't. "You think yourself smart, don't you?" they'd say. But I didn't; I only wanted people to laugh.

There sometimes wasn't a lot of laughing at our place; Mama wouldn't allow it. If you were done with your work, yes, you could read, or play jacks with your Cousin Gerda, if she was over; or you could sing *Komm Herr Jesu* in two parts, if Gerda wanted, or even Papa. Or you could even get the key from Mama and play organ, only it should be hymns or Strauss waltzes (the parts you knew of them), but don't you dare to play *There Was an Old Man and He Had an Old Sow* — they'd taught you it one time, over at Uncle Abe Schroeder's where people were laughers — but don't *you* try it; don't you and Gerda even try it unless Mama was out hoeing in the back garden and wouldn't hear you.

But the trouble was, by the time you got through all of Mama's chores, it was Sunday. And you daresn't get too funny on a Sunday; God might get mad.

It was a funny thing, but God didn't seem to, say if you had a birthday on a Sunday and you were old, thirty-six, and the grey was showing, a thread here and a thread there. And it was a busy time, spring seeding, but you had always had a birthday party at home where your folks were kind of modern because your mother was part English but came from out of the district far enough so that you never had to admit, never had to tell anybody your mother was part English before Opa made her a Uhrich and all at once so German she seemed to forget any other part.

But all the same, the birthday party part stuck, and so you had a birthday party, even married to a no-party man like Papa, some years on a Sunday. And you took a chance, I guess, on God getting mad.

God was good at it. If you didn't have your nickel out, let's say, for the red church velvet collection sack — beautiful, beautiful; you wanted to lay your cheek against it when it was passed down the row hanging like a bishop's cap (only really Herr Doktor Martin Luther's) — upside down at the end of its long velvet pole. Even the pole was red velvet, and Uncle Abe, Uncle Abe Schroeder or Uncle Abe

Uhrich, shoved it at you down the row. And supposing you
or Gerda didn't have your nickel out because you'd lost it,
or thought you'd get away with saving it for the school picnic by looking straight ahead as if you weren't there, Uncle
Abe Schroeder or Uncle Abe Uhrich just stood there, the
sack dangling in front of your nose, and finally they'd give
it a little shake, just a little one, and you felt God getting
mad and so you reached in the pocket of your second best
church dress — unless it was Easter or Christmas and then
you had a new one — and you took out your hankie with the
nickel tied tight in the corner of it, and undid the knot, it
was hard sometimes, and you let the nickel drop in the red
velvet sack, and then God wasn't mad any more.

And when you left the church that day, Uncle Abe
Schroeder would reach a hand to you and pull you to him.
And you would feel his one big hand fitting just warm and
nice there on top of your head, and then he would rumple
the curls there, Mama made them too tight some Sundays.
And he would say, "Growin like a weed," and pull you
closer to him yet, your face against his Sunday suit — it
always smelled nice, a little of horse and a little of tobacco
and a whole lot of Sunday and of church. But Uncle Abe
Uhrich would wag a finger a little under your nose, the
times you weren't quick to give your nickel; he would wag a
finger right under your nose, hoping I bet your mother
would see and ask what he was wagging it for.

But Mama never seemed to ask. She would just come
over and say, "Put your hat on, we're going; what's this
now, standing around in the church with no hat?" And if it
was a birthday Sunday she'd say then to Uncle Abe, "Come
by our place tonight, Abe, why don't you? And to bring the
fiddle would be nice."

And if it was Uncle Abe Schroeder, he would say, "Hoy-
yoy, it's that time-a-year again, is it? Somebody's gettin old,
hah?" But if it was Uncle Abe Uhrich, he would say,
"Maybe not this time." His own sister and yet he would

say, "Maybe not this time." And Mama would make a tight
mouth, she somehow made it always only on the left side of
the mouth; and she wouldn't say any more, only maybe,
"Well it's a drive home, and so we'd better go."

And Mama would make the same mouth when she was
telling Aunt Emma about it in the kitchen later. And Aunt
Emma, who was pretty good at shaking the finger sometimes, too, laughed a little and said, "Well, you know Abe
since he got married; he's almost afraid to breathe on Sundays. I don't know how she even lets him hitch up a horse
to go to church. I bet he has to leave the harness on over
Saturday night, don't you?"

And Mama would say, "On him or the horse?" And Aunt
Emma would say, "Both!" And then Mama would let loose
the tight lines of the mouth and laugh with Aunt Emma
and say, "It sure wouldn't surprise me."

They were in the kitchen; in Mama's kitchen. Mama and
Aunt Emma were in the kitchen putting doughnuts on big
platters and cutting sausage and brown bread and cold
pork, and mixing white curd skim milk cheese with sour
cream and chopped onion and paprika and sure not forget-
ting the salt. Only supposing the cheese was going out to
the heavy-laying hens, did you ever leave out the salt, and
then mostly you didn't bother to press the whey out of it,
even — what did the hens care? — you just curdled the milk
on the top of the warming oven or maybe even the back of
the stove, if you were careful and wouldn't burn it. And
then you poured it slop, slop — only be careful of your dress
if you were on your way to school — into the feeder pans for
the heavy-laying hens and, boy, did they ever like it.

But that was for hens. For people you pressed it out nice.
You pressed the white lumpy curds out nice and dry; some
even put a stone or at least a heavy plate on top and pressed
out all the whey, because nice and dry was better. Only,
you wet it all down again with sour cream and salted it and
put in lots of green onion tops if you had them in the

garden because it was summer. And if you didn't last until midnight when it was your mother's birthday, you better sneak some before you went to bed, because next day you could go check the milk cold house as soon as ever you got up, but there'd be none of it left.

Doughnuts there would be.

You didn't have to go to bed on your mother's birthday party if you didn't want to, but if you did there were lots of doughnuts left next day because she made lots. She made the doughnuts big. She made the dough in the bread *schüssel*, even, she made so many; and they rose big, like buns, before she even fried them in the hot lard.

Some she made with no holes; just cut out with the cookie cutter. She made a cut in the side with a skinny pantry knife and pried it apart a little with the same knife; then she dropped strawberry jam in, storebought, and closed it up again nice and tight to raise before frying. And for Mama the jam never leaked out when frying, but for my Aunt Emma, she didn't know how my mother ever did it, the jam always did.

Lots of people came to the party. Even Uncle Arnie Schroeder, who used to be quite a bit in love of Mama before she married Papa; I wasn't supposed to know that. And Uncle Arnie Schroeder should be ashamed of himself; he'd gone and let himself get conscripted and might even wind up shooting his own cousins down like dogs over there. It wasn't right; why didn't he apply for Cook at least in the army, but oh no, somehow Arnie Schroeder, Aunt Emma said, seemed to need to have a gun in his hands.

Not Papa. Papa had a twenty-two and he had the horse pistol. But Papa didn't like to shoot a duck, even, no matter how they ate away the barley.

You should have seen Uncle Arnie. He came all dressed up in his uniform, in his King George army uniform; showing off again, Aunt Emma said, who used to like him a lot the time when he was quite a bit in love of Mama: if you listen, you hear lots when you are in the kitchen washing dishes or folding away the dish towels.

And Uncle Arnie Schroeder's wife was an *Englishe*; she was from town; people said that's why he let himself get conscripted — because she was an *Englishe*, not because she was from town. Being from town didn't matter, only they could never milk and hardly ever wanted to learn, either.

Anyway, no matter what, Uncle Arnie had gone and got conscripted — some said he'd joined up, even — and so now all the brothers, Papa and Uncle Arnie had a quite a few of them, would have to push themselves and somehow farm for him, the little *Englishe* sure didn't know what end of a horse wore the bridle. Arnie would of been better to send her to town if he was gonna go off like that and shoot down his own cousins in a stupid war.

But they came to the party anyway, and the little *Englishe* was skinny and pinched looking, but my mama was a good nice armful and all pink and smiley with having a birthday party, even if it *was* on a Sunday.

Well, pretty soon Mama went over and sat for a while with the little *Englishe*, and told her not to worry because everything would turn out all right. A person just worked away hard day by day, Mama said, not looking for extra chores; just keeping up whatever had to be done, no matter what. And she had the gas washer, Mama said; good for her, or maybe good for Arnie; not everybody had one. And she had the cistern, no wash water to haul; that made a big difference. And Lucy and Marvin must be what, eleven, twelve, now? — my goodness, Marvin at least must be milking cows for two years already, not?

And the little *Englishe* got all wet-eyed and said Oh my, it wasn't the work; she was sure the boys would come up every day and be just as marvelous with the farm as Arnie; and Arnie had said at breakfast just this very day Albert would likely take the cows over to his place and keep track of the new calves that got born while Arnie was off fighting for King and Country.

As soon as ever she said Albert, Mama's eyes got their other look — like when you dared to say it wasn't your turn to get the day's wood in; right away, those times, her eyes got this other look and she said to you, "And just who else *is* there, Miss Madame, if you please?"

So now her eyes got that look. Uncle Arnie was Papa's spoiled little baby brother, that look said, and he thought he could have his own way about everything. And so Mama made that tight little straight line of the left side of her mouth and said, "Well I *suppose* that would work out. Are you milking more than six now?"

And that's when Uncle Arnie happened to come over to Mama. It was getting nearly midnight and he'd kept his nose in the schnapps ever since he came and so was laughing big and happy. He put his arm around Mama's shoulders and said, "How about a big birthday smackeroo, Queenie?"

And Mama said, "You had one already, the minute you came," and gave her shoulder a good wiggle to get his arm off.

Uncle Arnie just put his arm around her all over again and said, "Then how about a goodbye kiss? I might never see you again."

And Mama said, "Oh for goodness sake, Arnie, wait until you *go* someplace first." Because Uncle Arnie was just training yet. At Dundurn he was just training yet; you didn't need a ship or even a train to get there, somebody could take you there after morning milking and be back for dinner if they wanted to or tried.

And Mama got up, that half of her mouth tight; she wouldn't look at him, either. And right then Uncle Arnie just grabbed her where she stood and kissed her; he kissed her hard and for a long time; he was a awful big man and strong as Papa, I bet. Maybe more.

And ... well ... Mama maybe kissed him back a little, I

don't know; the little *Englishe* said later that she did. But
the fiddle stopped just then; Uncle Abe Schroeder's gold-
yellow fiddle stopped just then and so for sure everybody
saw them kissing and clapped and laughed about it.

And Mama by then had got a hand loose and was pound-
ing Uncle Arnie on the chest to quit it, quit it.

And people called to Papa, "Come see this, Albert, if you
want to learn how to say Happy Birthday good enough to
last for three years."

And Papa looked, and laughed, a little bit tight in the
throat, maybe, but he didn't go help. So I did.

I just all at once jumped onto Uncle Arnie's back from
halfway up the stairs where I was watching the party and
keeping awake so as not to miss the doughnuts and the
cream cheese. And I yelled, "Let her go, you sonofabitch!"
It was a good word; I liked it; I'd learned it from my friend
Albertina Bitner.

And Uncle Arnie yelled, "Hey!" and let go of Mama, but
not before I'd bit his ear good. Nearly off, he said. He was
lying; I never even tasted salt, hardly. It was a hot ear and
hard and big and hairy, and I don't know why I ever did it.

And everybody laughed. Well, not everybody. The little
Englishe said Uncle Arnie was mutilated and I was always
acting up and needed a good dose of discipline. And she
gave Uncle Arnie her silk handkerchief wet good with
schnapps to hold against his ear and he said "Christ,
Christ, Christ" after he jumped when she laid it on there.

And Papa came fast across the room and Uncle Arnie
said, looking right at Papa, "It's not funny, you know."

Papa stood there for a little minute. He looked at me and
I looked at him. He was sort of eating away at his top lip
with the under one and it seemed to me maybe he felt a little bit like crying.

Then he picked me up — I was really too big to get picked
up, already — and he held my face pressed snug against the
smooth sweated-up chest of his white Sunday shirt, and he

stroked my cheek with his other hand and said, "In *this* family we're raising us a tiger."

And everybody laughed again, but I didn't like it. It wasn't like at school when the big boys sometimes laughed at me being smart aleck and I liked it.

Then the fiddle started up again and Papa carried me into the kitchen. Mama was there already with Aunt Emma. Aunt Emma was standing bent over Mama. She looked up quick. Her face was all pink. Aunt Emma said to Papa, "Your brother is a pig; let him keep his hands where they belong." She said it just as if Papa was to blame for everything.

And Mama said to shush, what did it matter anyway. And Papa set me beside her on the bench alongside the table and told me, boy I'd sure shined my shoes good for Mama's party. He knelt to me to do and to say that.

And Mama blew her nose, right into her good Sunday hankie, and she said, "Oh well," and put her hankie away in a pocket. Then she turned to me and shook her head at me a time or two; she took my head in both her hands and made me look at her whilst she did that. "Such a big girl," she said, "and still such a tomboy. Whatever will we *do* with you?" And then she took her hands away; they were pretty cold hands, but they felt good there.

And Papa went back to the party; it was his job, he was supposed to be there. And Aunt Emma brought me a little dish of cream cheese and a doughnut, sugared and with store-bought strawberry jam inside. She brought cocoa, hot; she put cream in it from the Jersey cow to cool it.

And I sat beside Mama, the both of us not touching; she wasn't a one, much, to do that.

And the cream cheese looked nice, and the cocoa; and the doughnut had lots of sugar on it; but I couldn't even eat it.

And the water started coming into my eyes; and Aunt Emma said, "Come on now, don't you just sit and look at it. If you'd been in bed where you belonged, like a good girl, it never would of happened."

And so the water spilled over, and Mama said, "What? A big girl like you, and crying?"

And she lifted me onto her lap and hugged me. She wasn't ever a one to do that.

And it wasn't even *my* birthday.

We were going to see the king and queen after all. We were going because Miss Myse, she saw we got to do it. Miss Myse was fresh out of Normal School and those were the ones, so Francine Hoffer said, who weren't afraid to put theirselves out for people, not like Mr. Parsons last year or Mr. Orwell the year before, — wasn't that right, girls? — who used to come drunk from town, most Mondays, and then call them Krauts or even Squareheads all day long.

Miss Myse talked a whole lot about one's social duty and it took us a while to get cut in that *one* meant everybody. *Social duty*, nobody much thought about: it sounded like fun mixed with chores and jobs and I know my friend Albertina Bitner and I were ready to take our chances with it.

If going to see the king and queen was a *social duty*, boy, was that ever a good one. Miss Myse had made all the arrangements. She'd even got her boyfriend and his gravel truck to take us, twenty-seven Schroeders and Bitners and Hoffers and Montgomerys, to Saskatoon to see their royal imperial majesties. To see our royal British king and his beautiful British queen.

I was so happy I could hardly hold it. I'd written a whole nickel scribbler's worth of poems on the royal visit, which said I was glad they were coming in June in their car of maroon, because we'd all be in tune 'neath the silvery moon when we wended our way home from saluting them.

That car of maroon hit me in the mind hard, real hard, there in the part where it made the pictures; it hit me so hard I couldn't get over it. I thought of velvet. I thought and saw and smelled and felt warm velvet, the royal Christ's Lutheran church velvet. And I thought a maroon car should be honoured, right next to a king and a queen.

I was excited. The whole school was excited, even the six big boys in grade seven and grade eight. They were too old to be in school. They were fifteen, maybe sixteen even, because they got only about three or four months' school a year. The rest of the time they were hired men for their folks.

My friend Albertina Bitner and I heard them going on one day about the whole thing. It was the morning after Miss Myse had sent us all home with release forms for our folks to sign — in case the gravel truck turned over on the highway or something. Well, that was about the last thing that had to get done. "And so the arrangements," Miss Myse said, taking in the release forms the next morning, "are now as complete as need be, thank you all for being so marvelously prompt."

So we were ready. If your folks didn't sign, you might as well stay home from school that day, you wouldn't be going; Mr. Evans couldn't take a chance on you if you hadn't signed. Mr. Evans was Miss Myse's boyfriend, only she never called him that; she called him Mr. Evans but Francine Hoffer one time had seen them kiss.

So we were ready, and it was all anybody could talk about, even the big boys, who laughed sometimes about saluting the Union Jack in the mornings and singing *God Save the King*.

Miss Myse had talked so much, for so long, about the royal visit, there wasn't much time for arithmetic, who was sorry about that? And this one day the big boys were in the barn, the school barn, having their morning recess smoke. And my friend Albertina Bitner and I were in a back box-stall coaxing Canada, the Bitner's grey cart pony, with clover we'd picked for him, special, climbing through the school fence onto old Herschel Hoffer's land to do it.

The clover was very nice. It smelled a lot of clover when you picked it in the morning and it was still nice and wet.

Canada was nice. He was a little knock-kneed and pretty old, but he was a good horse, though not much interested in the gallop.

We were quiet in the box-stall with Canada and the quiet dark and the clover. It was very nice. But then the big boys came.

"Ach, it's nothin but politics," Louie Hoffer was saying when they all came in. Louie Hoffer thought he was the authority on every subject just because his Uncle Herman had gone back to Westphalia and was a file clerk in some government office there, one of the big girls once said. "There's gonna be a war, Pa says, sure as shootin," Louie Hoffer was saying, "and the Englishers just wanta wave the Union Jack, sending the Georgie-porjie and his Lizzie here, and get the stoopid Canadians all fired up, ready to get fed to the cannons."

Louie Hoffer took another drag on the cigarette he'd rolled from the butts in his pa's ashtrays and passed it on. I poked Albertina. I thought I should go and tell on them to Miss Myse — she wanted us girls to do it — only Albertina yanked me back with one hard yank and never even took her eyes off the see-hole in the wall of the box-stall to do it.

The big boys took turns stealing tobacco from home; everybody knew it. But Louie Hoffer's pa was so tight and so careful, he always carried just a small swatch around in his overall bib pocket and locked the rest of the tin in the sideboard, along with the silver coffee pot from Düsseldorf and the Sunday Bible with the copper clasps around its middle.

My Cousin Abe Schroeder coughed on his first drag of the smoke and said, "Oy-yoy, did you roll this outta dried horse apples or what?" and passed it on without a second drag.

And when he'd quit coughing and the others had taken a round or two apiece out of Louie for the bum tobacco, my Cousin Abe hawked his throat like the grown men smokers always did and then sent a good hard spit flying off to the side. And then he said *he* didn't care, so far as that went, about seeing any old king and queen, either; but he sure *was* interested in cosying up for a couple hours each way in the back of a gravel truck with Zenina Bitner and see could he get a grab at the queen's crown jewels.

"You sonofabitch," yelled my friend Albertina, and she tore out of Canada's box-stall so fast his poor old grey hairs stood up in the back-wind. And what could *I* do but light out after her where she'd taken Cousin Abe so by surprise she'd butted him right down into the manure and the straw. And for a minute there, I only more or less hopped around them, watching. I knew I should do something, but I didn't know what, so all at once I just jumped onto him, too, and sort of rode him anyplace that Albertina wasn't, and gave out once in a while with "Sonofabitch, long live the queen!" I was a little bit younger than Albertina, and pretty good, I guess, at confusing the issue.

Then Louie Hoffer — he was always a big bull and a strong one — he grabbed my friend Albertina up in his big hairy arms and held her, her back tight against his big belly and her feet kicking wild. And he said, smiling that smile he has whenever his ma gets him to drown a new batch of kittens, "Here ya are, guys. Line up; time ta press another Bitner inta service."

And I got up off Cousin Abe's head and ran at Louie Hoffer and kicked him hard in the ankle with my new kodiak field boots with the steel toes, and he yelled and let go of Albertina and said to me, "You little bitch. I'll mark you good with my pig knife."

So my friend Albertina and I tore for the barn door and Cousin Abe followed us out. Only Albertina wouldn't be caught dead running away from anybody, so she slowed, as soon as she got out the barn door, to a snappy walk. And I did, too; only I looked back over my shoulder all the while; but Albertina didn't.

And Cousin Abe caught up to us and walked too. And he said, talking low to Albertina, "Now listen Albertina, about Zenina ... about Zenina ... cross my heart and hope to die I never meant nothin. Honest to God I didn't. So don't tell her ... OK? OK?"

But my friend Albertina just swept along with her head held high like a queen. Or maybe a king, because the Bitner girls wore pants all the time. And she wouldn't so much as look at him.

"As if I'd tell her a thing like that," said my friend Albertina. "That Abe Schroeder is a horse's arse and then some." We were picking green maple leaves to put on our sandwiches for lunch. It was a lot like lettuce, so Albertina said. She knew a lot of things.

We generally ate alone, the two of us. The other girls in our grade said Albertina was big and dumb and always smelled of horses. But Albertina was not so dumb. She knew the names of every king of England since Arthur and was working hard, now, on the queens.

The other Bitner girls weren't stupid, either. It was just that they only got to school about as often as the grade eight boys. Maybe less. So how could they keep up with all that stuff about the Roman Empire, and about A working in a lumber camp for twice as long as B and one-half the recompense, so how much was the hourly wage of A compared to B?

Anyway, so I gave my friend Albertina my brown bread roast pork sandwiches loaded with maple leaf lettuce, and she let me have two of hers. This time it was white store bread again, spread with lard on one side and chocolate icing on the other. When I asked Mama for the same she just said, "Oh my goodness, what next?" and ignored me.

Albertina Bitner never ignored me. She listened. She read all my poems out loud, too, and said she wished she could sonofabitchin write stuff like that.

Albertina had the biggest blackest eyes you ever saw, but they always had clouds in them. I used to look away from them, sometimes.

Albertina was not a bad looker. The Bitner girls all looked like they'd been cut out with the same cookie cutter, Papa said once; and my Uncle Abe Schroeder said ya, the same baker, but not the same miller. And then they saw me in the next stall currying my horse Sermon, who did not have knock knees but was not as kind as Canada, and so they didn't say any more.

Nobody had to tell me about cookie cutters though. Anybody with half a brain could see that Albertina and Zenina and Sabrina and Ernestina all had the same heavy brown hair hanging straight down to the shoulders and the same white face with pain in it like the Mother Mary holding in her arms the Jesu just down from the cross. And they all had these lean, kind of cowpuncher bodies.

The little boys at home, there at the Bitners', were fat and dark and curly-headed. When I asked Papa once how come, he said he heard they ate lots of burnt toast there, why didn't I eat mine and try to be kruzzle-kopp, too. And for quite a while there, I believed it.

Sabrina and Ernestina did not go to school anymore. Their mother made them quit as soon as ever they were fifteen and the school inspector couldn't sic the Mounties on her. They helped with the field work and the chickens and cows, and they wore the same overalls all summer to save the time and water of washing. As soon as Zenina was done school, Ernestina was all set to go and get married; she just didn't know to whom, yet.

Zenina had one more year of school to go, and after that their mother would be holding her breath to see how quick she could get Albertina. But my friend Albertina said she'd sonofabitchin see them all in hell before *she* quit. Or maybe her old man, she said, would come home by then and at least he'd see she got to take the rest of school by correspondence.

Albertina's pa had been in Prince Albert ever since she was six years old. Nobody called it Jail or The Pen. They just called it getting sent to Prince Albert. A skinflint old widow had owed him a lot of hired man back wages and somehow he burned down an old house of hers, there down by the river. The trouble was — how could he know it? — the old lady just happened to be in it at the time.

"He usedta be in the army, back there for the old Kaiser," Albertina told me, taking large bites of pork sandwich and chewing wide so that her tongue showed like pale pink liver amongst it. I looked the other way.

"You shoulda seen him salute," said Albertina, using a finger to pick out some meat caught in her teeth. I wondered if I should remind her of the germs Miss Myse had told us about that loved to find safe harbour under the nails of negligent boys and girls who ignore the golden rules of health. But I remembered just in time how Albertina had said she got enough sonofabitchin rules at home and she flipped her *Golden Rules of Dental Safety* into Canada's manger when we hitched up to drive home that day.

Lots of times my Cousin Abe would help hitch up if it

was Zenina's turn to try to get Canada between the shafts of the pony cart, but after that day in the barn he never came near. It was OK by my friend Albertina and me, and that's for sure. But somehow it didn't seem to be OK with Zenina.

She used to watch him with those clouded Bitner Mother Mary eyes whilst he yanked his shagannapi's tether chain where he was staked out across from the school barn; she watched while he sprang atop him to charge across the prairie like the Lone Ranger off to save a widow. My Uncle Emil Schroeder used to say that about Cousin Abe. My Uncle Emil Schroeder called Cousin Abe that young pup, and didn't care who heard him. Cousin Abe was Uncle Abe Schroeder's young pup. Uncle Abe and Uncle Emil didn't seem to like each other much. They were brothers. They were Papa's brothers. They both seemed to like Papa OK, but nobody really ever told me. I liked Cousin Abe Schroeder pretty well, except when my friend Albertina didn't seem to like him.

And anyway, no matter what, it was getting to be the time of the royal visit. And when Albertina and I made plans about how we were going to hold our Union Jacks right over our hearts as the king and queen drove by in their car of maroon, and when we talked about how Miss Myse would take us on a tour of Palm Dairies where they might give us a free ice cream cone apiece — black licorice, if you can imagine; Miss Myse had had one there once — Zenina kept her sad and clouded eyes on the shagannapi's dust on the trail ahead and did not talk about the royal visit.

We might even get a formal tour through Eaton's, Miss Myse had said, since we had a place reserved for us outside the store to view their majesties and she knew the manager. You'd think Zenina went to Saskatoon every day of her life, she ignored it so; even the part where we were liable to get to ride once apiece up the Eaton's escalator.

All that would happen if we were being quite orderly,

Miss Myse said. Miss Myse had read somewhere that Germans loved order and she always seemed a little bit insulted that the big boys were so smart aleck about it. It was like they had never heard that Germans love order. Or maybe they didn't know they were Germans, though Miss Myse said lots of times they were. Anyway, they did not like a lot of rules. And when they got forbade the coal shed, they set a pee-in-a-bottle trap for her above the door, and argued about who would get to supply the pee for it.

But Albertina saw them set it above the coal shed door. And she went and leaned in through the broken window at the back, and she pitched a rock at it and broke it. And sure enough, Miss Myse heard it and came out and thought Albertina had broken the window. And who was gonna tell about a sonofabitchin pee-in-a-bottle, so Albertina got held up as a sad example in Civic League meeting that Friday; it wasn't even fair.

Miss Myse talked tight-lipped about the Bitner girls to Mama that night, when she came to borrow her Ontario School Curriculum, the Saskatchewan one having made its way down the boys' toilet hole when Louie Hoffer helped his ma whitewash the coal sheds and toilets that summer.

Anyway, so it got to be the morning of the day of the royal visit. Mama made me wear my white flower girl's dress, the one from Cousin Bernice Schroeder's wedding, in honour of the queen. And Papa loaned me the Union Jack he kept stuck in the back of the Wheat Pool calendar, in honour of the king. The Board of Trade in Saskatoon sent little Union Jacks out to all the schools. Miss Myse handed them out the day before, each one rolled up neat as neat and with a rubber band around it. But Papa's was bigger.

Mama made him drive me to school in the Sunday buggy, "Otherwise she'll for sure take a lift with you-know-who and wind up with manure on her skirt yet." By eight o'clock it was already hot, and when we got there all the girls were swinging around in their summer picnic dresses with their hair all crimped from rag rollers or hot iron wavers, whilst the boys scuffed their Sunday oxfords in the dust as if it didn't matter and ran fingers around the necks of tight shirt collars to get a little air.

And then the Bitner girls arrived. "Late as usual," Francine Hoffer said, right out loud as they drove in. Both of them were wearing brand new overalls with the red GWG on the bib pocket.

"Overalls, can you imagine! What will people think?" said Francine Hoffer. She was Queen of the May that year and, ever since, she wanted everything to look real nice. Then she bent over to me and straightened the sash in place around my middle and gave it a little pat and said, "Isn't this one a doll, girls? A perfect Eaton's Beauty!" And I felt beautiful, all of a sudden, like a princess at court, almost; and I liked the idea quite a lot.

There was Miss Myse then, scolding the Bitners to do get a move on, Mr. Evans has had the motor running for three minutes waiting for you. And everybody got real quiet all of a sudden with the excitement of being ready. And Francine Hoffer said again, "Bib overalls of all things! To see the queen!" And Albertina's face got all pink like the heart inside old beets, and she gave poor old Canada the buggy-whip the rest of the way to the barn.

Nobody went down to help them unhitch. I thought of it, but then I was glad to remember my white flower girl's dress and Mama and the chance of manure, and so I didn't.

The rest of us filed orderly into the gravel truck backed up to the schoolhouse steps. Mr. Evans stood at the tail-gate and handed the girls in quite gallant.

Francine got handed in before anybody else: she stood herself in line first. She was the Queen of the May that year and so she knew how to do things. And Miss Myse stood by and said "Hurry along now, everyone" every now and again to show she had everything in order. So people filed in fast and quiet. Only I didn't have to file because Francine Hoffer called to her brother Louie, "Lift the Eaton's Beauty up over the side, Lou; I want her here on my lap, she's so precious."

And Miss Myse didn't contradict Francine; Francine was the Queen of the May and her papa was the chairman of the schoolboard.

And Louie Hoffer picked me up in his big hands with the black hair all over them. And I'd rather he had stuck me with the pig knife. I hated Louie Hoffer's hands. It was not so much the missing thumb he'd shot off with the twenty-two, it was something to do with the way that he drowned kittens.

He swung me so high over his head so fast, I got the horseback ride tingles in my stomach and lower down too. You get the same thing when you go too high on the swings and come down with a rush against the wind. If there is no one else around, it is a good feeling.

And Francine put me on her lap and held me. And everybody started to talk and laugh because they knew we were really going to go now — we were going to have for sure an adventure.

And the big girls called, "Oh Miss Myse, this is so *love-ah-lee*." It was a word Miss Myse liked a lot too, right next to order. And Miss Myse looked quite pleased and gave the big girls a little wink as if to say they'd get their chance to organize things, too, some day.

But then she called all the more across to Albertina and to Zenina running up the hill from the barn, "*Will* you get a move on!" And she said to Mr. Evans, "Why not put up the tail-gate and get in the cab now, Jim? Overalls can climb over."

And Mr. Evans got a kind of funny look on his face but he did it; he was, after all, a boyfriend. And Albertina and Zenina panted up, their faces white and little drops of sweat standing around on the nose and the forehead.

And the motor raced. And Zenina's eyes were clouded. And Cousin Abe Schroeder reached down over the side and hoisted her up and in like she was a doll, he did it so easy. He grabbed her and lifted her in and folded his good suit-coat for her to sit on and gave her his Sunday hankie with the blue embroidered A on it to wipe her face on. And he glared around at everybody like a she-coyote standing watch over a new litter.

Albertina fell in over the side just as Mr. Evans spun his wheels in the gravel for the take-off. "Sonofabitch," she said. But she did not look at anybody. She took her broken Union Jack out of her bib overall pocket and turned her back and stood there alone at the back of the gravel truck and looked backwards all the way to town, like a cow-puncher watching the trail behind when someone else is do-ing the driving.

And Francine Hoffer held my hand all day in the city and the big girls called me her princess. And when the king and queen came by in a big black Cadillac with a motorcycle escort so thick you could hardly see them, I never once thought about how we'd been told it was going to be a car the colour of French wine.

I forgot to hold Papa's Union Jack over my heart even, like we'd planned. But when Louie Hoffer swung me up on his shoulder to see better, his hot hands getting tighter and tighter on me as he held me, I saw Albertina take a step out into the street. Her broken Union Jack was pinned to the front of her new bib overalls. She clicked the heels of her scuffy field boots to attention with a slap as the royal limousine passed by and, eyes front, she snapped into a salute and held it.

Miss Myse told her as we were loading for home, that it was an unseemly display and had drawn unflattering attention to the entire group.

"Sonofabitch," said Albertina.

And she would not eat any of the peanuts Miss Myse had bought for us to have on the way home.

When it got to be December, Uncle Abe Schroeder was liable to come by with the mail and say, to wink at me in Mama's kitchen and say, "Well now, what do you know, it's pretty near time for *der Peltznikel* to come around again and I wonder, do we have here somebody who was good enough all year for a switch, or good enough for chocolate candies, or what?"

"Chocolate candies, Uncle Abe," I'd say. And sure enough, he'd have some in his pocket for me; he'd just come from town, the snow was awful deep, he said, he only just hoped *der Peltznikel* was gonna make it through the drifts when the time came.

I thought Mama wasn't listening. She had her head down to the mending and she had her mouth set like she wasn't listening, only just waiting for some talker to quit talking so she could say *her* say.

"I wish you would quit it with the *Peltznikel*, Abe," Mama said. "They get enough Santa Claus, Santa Claus, Santa Claus in that school, seems to me, without hearing it at home too, as soon as it's time to get ready to put on the school Christmas concert. Can't you do a person a favour and tell her it's time for Jesu the Christus to be born again, instead of always that stuff about the *Peltznikel?*"

"Come on now, open up," Uncle Abe said to me. So I did, and he dropped another chocolate candy, whole, into my mouth. This one had a cherry right in the middle of it. It was the best kind.

"The only ones who get born again are the Christians, Tina," Uncle Abe said. "Once was once too much for the Lord God Jesu, it seems to me sometimes. And people can say all they want to say, but sometimes there's a lot more good comes out of *der Peltznikel* than comes out of getting born again into a Christian."

Mama made that mouth.

"Come on now," Uncle Abe said, "don't make that mouth at me. Sometimes, honest to God, I think it's just too bad the Roman lions didn't eat us all up, back in the old days, then we wouldn't be telling each other all the time some of us aren't living right and better get born again — and before we even die the first time, for God's sake, from scarlet fever or the lions. Yessiree," Uncle Abe would say, meanwhile sorting through the mail he'd dropped on the kitchen table, and putting his to one pile and ours to another pile, "yessiree, it sometimes seems to me there's a lot more good comes out of der good old *Peltznikel* than a whole churchful of getting born again."

Uncle Abe was like that. Mama couldn't talk him down the way she could Papa. Uncle Abe just changed the subject around enough to make you think you were still talking about what you started in on, and then he talked so quick and so earnest about it, it sounded like good sense even after he was done talking.

Mama was a talker and Uncle Abe Schroeder was a talker. And Mama was something else, too. Mama was the kind could get miffed over anything and anybody. Maybe a person shouldn't say it, but over Uncle Abe Schroeder, somehow, Mama just seemed to laugh and say he was a pretty poor influence on the younger generation, how about some coffee before he went home, and how about it, didn't he bring *her*, too, some chocolate drops?

"Sure thing," Uncle Abe always said. "Come on now, open up." And she did, and sometimes he dropped in three whole candies and said "*Now* who's got a big mouth?" but she'd just hold a hand over the mouth to keep the candies in and go get the coffee.

And when she went Uncle Abe would say, "Come on, you're not too big to sit on a knee; come and tell me what I'm supposed to say the next time I see *der Peltznikel.*"

And it was a funny thing, it always seemed about the time Uncle Abe stopped by with the mail, winters, and started to talk about the *Peltznikel*, pretty soon next thing in school Miss Schwartz, or before her, Miss Myse, started to talk about the school Christmas concert, and who would have to do what for it.

I never wanted to do anything. I just wanted to sit in the congregation — no, in the audience; congregation is for church, Miss Elda Schwartz said so. (I bet she used to say congregation herself before she went away to Normal School and got to be a teacher.) But now Elda Schwartz was a real stickler for the right word; she had to be: she was a teacher in the very same school where the teachers were always good, Elda Schwartz told us lots of times, at teaching you the right words so that you could live in the world with civilized people and not be ashamed of your origins.

Miss Schwartz cared a whole lot about words. She seemed to care a whole lot about living right too. And when she learned how to be a teacher she somehow learned how to think up things like a doggone Swear Can to catch people out who said so much as a *Shucks* or a *Darn* when they fell off a swing or tripped each other up on the schoolgrounds.

Lucky she didn't have a Spoke German Today Can. We'd all have been in it.

If Elda Schwartz had had a Spoke German Today Can we'd all have been in it, because when she wasn't out on the ball diamond, recess, we spoke German no matter how much she preached about the Mounties liable to come out checking.

She didn't have a Spoke German Today Can. I guess she never thought of it, she was too busy thinking about having a Swear Can.

And Elda Schwartz had been told often enough by the pastor that even words like *Shucks* and *Darn* were just as bad as the words they were a shortcut for, so even for words like *Shucks* and *Darn* you could make the sayer have to stand up in class in Civic League meeting, Fridays when the Swear Can was opened, and the people who'd got caught had their names read out. And the sayer would have to stand up and say, "Forgive me Lord and Miss Schwartz and the pupils of Blenheim School for saying *Shucks* on the schoolgrounds."

If you'd said *Lord God Jesu* or *Crap* or *Bugger off*, it was the same thing — you had to say the bad word when you stood up; you had to say the bad word so that you would be shamed having to say it. I had to do it lots, but I was only ashamed for getting caught out over it.

Guys like John Peters and Otto Uhrich, they never got ashamed over anything. They would say, "Listen to me, Helga!" whenever Helga Uhrich was around — Helga Uhrich was a tattle tale and could be counted on to put your name in the Swear Can if you so much as screwed up your mouth to spit. And John Peters and Otto Uhrich, they'd say a terrible something right to Helga Uhrich's face — she was a cousin to both of them and her mother didn't like their mothers.

Mostly John Peters and Otto Uhrich said a dirty something — they didn't go so much for the *Lord God Jesu* — they would say it to Helga just so they could get to stand up in class and say they were sorry and say the word all over

again right there in Civic League meeting and then snigger
about it afterwards.

The Swear Can was mostly in summer. It was mostly in
summer when people were outside on the ball diamond and
Miss Schwartz wasn't. Miss Elda Schwartz, I bet, thought
a teacher belonged behind the teacher's desk, because she
hardly ever left there.

In winter she had to. In winter she had to get out the
music and the recitation pieces from the locked cupboards,
and she'd have to get out the play books and decide who
had to do what for the Christmas concert.

Miss Schwartz decided. After the first year she got to be
the teacher Miss Schwartz always decided. It was only the
first year she had a vote on it. The first year we had Miss
Schwartz there was a vote on everything. She was just fresh
out of Normal School and she got taught Psychology there
and everything, to tell her how to have votes on everything.
The trouble was, voting made everything such a shemozzle
because everybody wanted to be Santa Claus or Mrs. Santa
Claus and nobody wanted to be a reindeer or elf with nothing much to say or do, only stand there.

Except me. Mostly everybody else wanted to say and to
do lots. And whoever heard of a Christmas concert play,
Miss Schwartz said, with ten Santas and ten Mrs. Santas
and only one reindeer or elf? Nobody would write a play
like that, Miss Schwartz said, it wouldn't make sense; it
would be stupid.

So I guess that's how Miss Schwartz decided she would
be the one who decided who would do or be what, and I
had a dry mouth all the while it took her to do that, in case
she said I had to be or do something. My mind didn't want
it. It only wanted to sit out with Papa and Mama and see
the school all lit up with candles and with two gas mantle
lamps; to see the red and green paper bells hanging from
red and green streamers looped in waves criss-cross over-
head from the school ceiling's four corners; my mind

wanted to see and hear the people call out Hello to late-comers from the front grade one and two desks where the firstcomers squeezed themselves to see the stage best because they'd had the good sense to come early.

My mind just wanted to see and smell and hear it all: the people and the colours and the candle wax and the soft fizz-fizz-fizz of the gas mantle lamps, the candies and the Jap oranges leaking their smells out of the brown paper sacks stacked in bushel potato baskets under the Christmas tree, the real piney Christmas tree brought from town and decorated by the schoolboard after we went home from dress rehearsal the afternoon of the concert.

My mind just wanted to keep it all; keep it all inside, somewhere, or else spinning outside around and around the head — like a ring of light around and around the head, like the ring of light that spun and rang and shone around the head of the holy mother and the Lord God Jesu in the pictures on the catechism cards you learned by heart because you had to learn them, or else.

And another thing, after you had learned the cards by heart and said them, you better pretend you were glad when they gave you a *St. John Testament* for saying them.

My mind was a funny one, maybe. It just wanted to be there and see and smell and hear it all. And be really glad, not pretend glad. And feel it all. And *be* it all, somehow. And then keep it all, all, so that it could give you back the pieces — the pictures, the smells, the sounds: all the pieces — and so make it whole for you again when you got home after the concert and Mama put a hot water bottle with you under the feather tick so you would warm up fast. And you lay there, the smell of peanuts and Jap orange still on your fingers, and it was like the whole concert was happening again inside you and around you until all at once it was turned into a dream because you slept.

That was the way of it if you could just be there at the concert and not have to do anything. But then there came

this one concert time when I had to be the Mrs. Santa
Claus because the part had lots of lines to speak and I could
really do that. Miss Schwartz said so.

She said right. I could. I didn't want to; my mind didn't
want it; but I could do it, fast and good. So I had to take the
book home and copy out the part. You didn't have to copy
out the whole thing. In fact, you daresn't do that. If you did
that and the Mounties caught you, you could get made to
go to court, and that would cost you or your papa lots of
money — worse than the Mounties catching you talking
German on the ball diamond. If you got caught copying the
whole play book it wouldn't cost you jail, it would cost you
worse: it would cost you lots of money — or your papa, if
you didn't have any.

So anyway, I had to take the book home and copy out all
of Mrs. Santa's part in a good scribbler. And I had to put in
there, too, the last few words said by the one who spoke
ahead of her in the book, like Santa or maybe a reindeer.

It took a long time to do.

And this one particular time, Mama said to Papa,
"Maybe take pity on her and help her write it. I have to get
started on the angel *cost-yooms* tonight, I promised Miss
Schwartz."

One thing about Mama, she would never call Elda
Schwartz Elda Schwartz, now she was the Blenheim School
schoolteacher. Mama knew the way that was proper, even
though she'd had Elda Schwartz in catechism class years
ago and told Papa when she heard she was coming to be the
schoolteacher that Elda Schwartz was not liable to be too
bright unless she'd grown a lot more brain since Mama
sweated the catechism into her in Saturday catechism class
in church.

"Ten angel *cost-yooms* again this year!" Mama said.
"Wouldn't you think they would try to keep at least a few
over, year to year? But oh no, if somebody will sew their
eyes out on angel *cost-yooms* year after year, what does it

matter to them?"

As soon as ever Mama told Papa to help me, I'd quit writing and just sat there and listened to her. Papa still sat with his pipe and his paper; you'd think he was reading and not listening. It was sometimes easy to wish you could learn to do that too.

"It's a long part, this Mrs. Santa Claus part," Mama said, rolling white crepe paper off the roll in a long white wave across almost the whole long kitchen table. "It's really such a long part for somebody Alvena's age, but Miss Schwartz says she can do it."

That's when Papa put down his pipe and his paper and came and sat down beside me, and so you knew he'd been listening after all and that it would all turn out all right. He took the book, the play book, and my scribbler too, but I stayed right there beside him, hunkered right there beside him, to watch him get the words right, in case he missed some or wrote too many and so might have to go to court for it. And he would turn to me every now and again while Mama was talking, and he'd raise his eyebrows, both at the same time, as if he was saying "Well what do you think about that?" while she said all the rest.

"Miss Schwartz says Alvena is so good at it, it will make the whole play if Alvena does it," Mama said. "She's gonna get a real big Santa to play against her. To make it funnier. A real big Santa and a real little Mrs. Santa. People will think it's real cute, Miss Schwartz says. Can't you just hear people laughing," Mama said, eyeing up the wave of white tissue paper and picking up the scissors, "when Mrs. Santa Claus turns out to be our little Alvena here, and Santa turns out to be that big barrel of a Louie Hoffer?"

"She'd never!" I said. I jumped right out of my chair, right against Papa's writing arm, too, so that his pencil, it was a real dark black one, marked the whole page almost corner to corner in one long black mark, right across the written words and everything. "She'd never make it Louie

Hoffer," I said, or maybe I hollered it. "She'd never! He isn't even in school anymore."

If it was Louie Hoffer, why, they could take me to jail for talking German and I'd be glad about it; I'd talk German right in classtime all day tomorrow. If it was Louie Hoffer, they could take me to court for copying all the play book; when Papa went to bed tonight, saying it was done, I would take the book and copy and copy in my room, and get up early if I had to and copy some more so that I could get it all down and go to court instead of having to be Mrs. Santa and have Louie Hoffer kiss me hello and goodbye every other page of that play book.

"Just simmer down, young madame," Mama said, "was I speaking to you? Was I? When I am speaking to you then you can have a say." She patted the white crepe paper, some cut and some not cut yet; she was looking for the scissors that had got itself lost on her again. "You've got to hand it to that young Louie," she said to the crepe paper. "To go back to school and try to get his Eight, that's no easy thing by no means. I'm only surprised," Mama said, having found the scissors and starting to cut again, "I'm only surprised a Hoffer has it in him to do that."

"Well I don't know," Papa said, "you're sure Elda Schwartz isn't the attraction, and not the Grade Eight?" He was erasing the marks the pencil had made when I bumped him, and he was tracing in the missing parts of letters again after erasing. And one part of my mind said, Good for Papa, it will be neat still, but another part of me could only see Louie Hoffer grabbing me up in his red Santa suit close against his private parts to kiss me once every other page.

That's the way he did it. He had the part of Mr. Whippletree once, in a play that was supposed to be funny. And Louie Hoffer wasn't as big and round and strong as any bull then yet, but when he grabbed Hedy Uhrich on Christmas concert night and kissed her because Mr. Whippletree was making up a fight with Mrs. Whippletree about the new hat she bought that cost twenty-seven dollars, he held her, he held Mrs. Whippletree — being, of course, Hedy Uhrich — held her, so she told Donelda Hoffer later, so tight against his private parts she could feel everything he had.

Everybody laughed. Guys whistled and old men and women laughed their big belly laughs, the ones that were big and had big bellies to laugh out of. Some of the mothers only laughed little thin laughs, like maybe they were wondering, supposing it was their girl up there on the stage getting held so close it made people laugh to see it; but mostly they laughed to see big Louie Hoffer grab Hedy Uhrich to him and kiss her in a real long kiss; kiss her the way real kissers kissed, not with a pretend kiss like they had practiced up on, faces turned to the backdrop and not to the people who watched.

And after that Christmas concert, sometimes Louie Hoffer and Hedy Uhrich kissed a whole lot in the cloakroom too. And then pretty soon Hedy Uhrich quit school and went on holidays to her auntie in Arnprior, way down in Ontario, and she never came back for a long time, I guess she was having too good a time.

One time before that, before Hedy Uhrich went on holidays to her auntie and even before the school Christmas concert when Louie Hoffer first kissed her, my friend Albertina Bitner and I drove up to Louie Hoffer's pa's farm because Francine Hoffer told us their barn cat had just had kittens again, seven, all of them as white as snowballs, and cuter than a bug's left ear. Everything was cuter than a bug's left ear to Francine Hoffer just then, but I knew if it was kittens they'd be pretty cute all right.

And when we heard about it, Albertina said she'd drive right after school first south to Hoffers' for the kittens, then quick as could be past the school and on to our place and home if I thought I could get away with being dropped off

at our gate a hour late, and if I knew a way of taking home
unbeknownst to Papa or Mama a new kitten that could
scarcely yet hold open its eyes.

"I'm gonna get two," I said. And all day I could hardly
wait.

But when we stepped into the Hoffers' kitchen and called
"Hoo hoo! Anybody home?" nobody answered for a minute. And then Mrs. Hoffer called, "Out here, out here, out
here!" from behind a little shed where she was picking
geese. And when we said we'd come for the kittens, she
said, "Oh them. I told Louie to take them to the horse
water trough and drown them. There's too many cats on
this place as it is."

Well, Albertina and I ran quick as we could to the horse
water trough. And Louie had four mewling white kittens
left in the milk pail and he had three wet ones dead, laid out
on a big manure shovel to bury when he was done. And we
begged him for the others, for even two, one, of the others.
But Louie Hoffer just laughed and said, "Nah! What do
you want with a white snowball in summer? It'll just melt
away on you in the hot sun."

And then he took another mewling white kitten up out of
the milk pail in his big fat hand, thumb and finger around
the kitten's throat, only not squeezing off the mewl — he
seemed to like to hear that — and dunking the white kitten
slow, slow, into the water of the horse water trough, not
taking his eyes off the way it mewled and wiggled and tried
to claw the air with its little toenails. And he didn't hold it
there long; he brought it up again to see if it still mewled, I
guess, because when it did, he laughed a little and said,
"Want some more, ya little bugger?" and dipped it under
the water again and when he pulled it out again it didn't
mewl anymore.

And somehow we watched him do that one and reach for
the milk pail to get the next one. Only that's when my
friend Albertina grabbed the milk pail and ran, and ran,

and beat Louie Hoffer to the pony cart, and jumped in, and slapped up the pony, and dumped the kittens out on the straw of the pony cart, and threw the milk pail back towards Hoffers' into the ditch, and just kept agoing down the road.

And Louie Hoffer stopped and turned around and there was me pelting up, but did I ever put on the brakes because Louie Hoffer was looking at me like I was a white kitten and I'd be the one he drowned next. Only his ma, she came out from behind the shed all over goose feathers, and she asked .what was all the commotion, didn't Louie have enough to do? if not, she'd see to it he got busy picking geese here in a minute.

And Louie offer said, "The Bitner kid made off with three of the young ones before I could drown 'em."

And Mrs. Hoffer said, "What do *you* care? There's three less then for you to waste your time on, and just as many less begging milk in the milk barn in the next little while."

Then she asked me did Mama send me over for anything else besides kittens. And I said No. Then she asked me were the kittens maybe for Mrs. Bitner, not for Mama. And I said Yes.

Then she said, "Well Louie, you take Albert Schroeder's little girl right on home, since that Bitner one wouldn't wait. Such manners. As if she couldn't wait a minute or get a little milk here to see them home, not gallop a horse in the sun home because she had a handful of new kittens to baby. But then," Mrs. Hoffer said, "what could you expect of Elmyra Bitner's brood? They had no bringing up to speak of."

So anyway, Louie Hoffer went and got his saddle horse and I had to get up in front, tight in the saddle with him. And he held his one hand too close down on me, to hold me. And when I tried to move it up, he just held tighter and dug his fingers in and said, "Now now, tickle-tickle, little Pickle."

When he caught up to Albertina he said, "Give me back them kittens and I'll let her go."

Albertina looked up at me and I made a mouth to say No.

So Albertina said, "Ride her all the way to Albert Schroeder's, if you got time on your hands. Your Ma will save the chores for you and make you some more besides for being late; I heard already how she runs things."

And Louie Hoffer swore and reached down to grab the bridle on Albertina's cart horse.

So Albertina grabbed up the buggywhip and let him have it right across the face.

And I fell off Louie Hoffer's saddle horse and should have broke something, I guess, only I didn't.

And Albertina kept laying on the buggywhip, and Louie Hoffer's saddle horse kept trying to climb into the buggy or into the harness with Albertina's cart horse.

And then I heard one of the kittens mewling. So I got up off the ground quick, and climbed into Albertina's cart from the back and said, "Go!" And Albertina did.

She stopped at the road gate at our place behind the saskatoon berry bushes there, and we brushed me off. And she had a couple of safety pins she kept pinned all the time to the bib pocket of her overalls, in case, so she used them to do up a tear in my skirt in hopes Mama wouldn't notice it till wash day. And we took the kittens around the back way and into the barn, and we put them into a manger.

When we got to the house, there was a note from Mama saying she'd gone to church to a meeting, so go right out to where Papa was cultivating summerfallow and ride around with him until supper.

She didn't say, Change clothes.

So Albertina and I, we got some milk and warmed it for the kittens, and helped them dab-dab-dabble it down; it took an awful long time, but it was kind of nice to do that.

Then Albertina drove me to the field to Papa. She wasn't worried about getting home late. She said her ma would believe anything, and wouldn't much care, so long as the pony wasn't brought home winded.

And Papa stopped the horses to let me climb up on the cultivator with him and said, "Well now, maybe you should have put on overalls for this dirty job here; what will Mama say if you come home with a tear in this nice blue dress?"

And I said, "Maybe it won't get one." And Papa said, "Well now, that's the way to talk." And then we started moving and I told him about the kittens. And Papa said, "Well well — whoah, Jess! — you're sure bound and determined to be a mother, now aren't you? — Go, Jess! — Now maybe we just won't bother mentioning them new white kittens to Mama for a few days, how's about that?"

I didn't tell about Louie Hoffer. Everything in my mind said not to bother telling any of the parts about Louie Hoffer.

So anyway, that time about the school Christmas concert: Mama tried to help me learn the Mrs. Santa part for the play, and Papa tried to help me learn it too. But every time I read the words or heard the words, I saw inside me and outside me, somehow, Louie Hoffer drowning kittens in the water of the horse water trough.

Then right away I got sick inside my head and I couldn't learn the words: there were words there already, hot inside my head, and they were saying Don't you ever learn those words.

And Miss Schwartz said in school she didn't know what had come over me, and if I couldn't get the words down pat to practice with Louie by end of the week, she'd have to give the part to somebody else.

I forget now who it was got the part.

When my Aunt Ruby was married was a good time for everybody but my Aunt Ruby. She was my Aunt Ruby then already, in a kind of a way, but people didn't call her that. Pretty soon she had a baby, a pink and white baby in a clothes basket, sucking his thumb and looking up at you milky and smiling around it; but I never knew she was a aunt — I thought she was a hired girl — until after she got married.

The baby had a father but it never knew it because my Uncle Walter was gone to the war by then, being a soldier and hoping he'd meet his Cousin Gustav, the one he was still sore at and who went back to the old country and was fighting with a gun to show the world the race was pure, so the papers said. Only Mama's Cousin Gustav wasn't like that, Papa said. Mama's Cousin Gustav used to say his great-grandmother was a Jew and, being dead for too many years, nobody who counted knew it to make trouble, but she'd been the best blood into that whole family in two hundred and fifty years.

And Mama said Hitler was stupid and so was her Cousin Gustav to go back there, but Papa said how could the man help himself — he loved Bavaria.

And I was surprised. You didn't say love around our place, it was a kind of a word you saved for God and if you ever said it you kept it holy and said it in German.

Love, said Uncle Walter, and surprised me twice in a row, Love for corn's sake. Uncle Walter was a soldier, Mama's baby brother soldier, who said of course he never joined up just because Papa's baby brother did. And Uncle Walter was a soldier who would point his gun, he said, laughing, at his Cousin Gustav if he ever saw him, and blow his brains out, and it didn't have anything to do with a pure or unpure race, it had to do with the time his Cousin Gustav took his pants down for him and whipped his bare behind for not killing the gophers before he cut their tails off for the bounty.

Uncle Walter wasn't mean anymore, but he was a good hater. He was a good liker, too, but you better be careful. If he was in a kissing mood, you had to get out of the way or he'd grab you and tickle you and kiss you smack dab on the lips, yukk, and whisker rub you, and when he caught you running past him he'd grab you up under the armpits and his hands would stay on your chest things, and he'd move his fingers over and over the two pimple spots and go yum-yum-yum into the back of your neck, making tingles go skittering like crazy up and down your back whilst you hollered Ma!

And Mama would come and say, Walter you cut that out; you'll make the kid nervous. And he'd tickle harder and the two pimple spots would get tingly and your breath would come in whoops and your heart would pound for the wishing to get free out of the cage of his hands.

And Mama would say again, Walter! standing there in the doorway stirring the cake batter in the mixing bowl she'd brought along so as not to waste time. And her voice would be like when you thought you'd gotten by with sneaking out when she'd told you to fill the wood-box. And Uncle Walter would say, Say *Please* then, Petunia. And I wouldn't. Somehow I just wouldn't. To say *Please* for your own heart was a thing I couldn't do. I just hollered louder and kicked and threw my arms with fists in circles and just before I had to holler Sonofabitch in front of Mama — the razor strap was always handy — somehow Papa would come in the door asking for the hot mash for the hens or to see were the milk pails scalded and ready.

And Uncle Walter would drop me so fast I sometimes fell, but I got up fast, never mind the scrapes, and ran and got behind Papa. And Papa would reach behind himself and find my hand and pull me out and say, I think you better come carry out the milk pails. And he'd say, Milking done your place already, Walter? My, you're quick.

And Walter would say, If you got a good hired girl you don't need no clock to milk by. And that was Aunt Ruby; the clock was Aunt Ruby who wasn't my Aunt Ruby yet; and Papa would say Phfumpf into his moustache and we'd go out.

And then Uncle Walter came back one day wearing a army uniform and looking beautiful, and Mama cried and said, You'll get shot and killed; oh Walter why did you do it? And he said then about his Cousin Gustav, about his and Mama's Cousin Gustav, and I said inside myself — or another part of me did — I hope he sees you first!

That hearing part was awful. It was like hearing yourself — only not you but somebody more important — sort of deep inside your ears, inside the head, and it scared me there for a minute. And that night I had a dream, with Uncle Walter beautiful in it in his new army uniform, and he was reaching for me and smiling with large white teeth that shone and sparkled so close I could see his tongue meaty and pink and the inside of his mouth wide open and wet and laughing. And my heart was caught in the cage of not wanting to be tickled, and Papa came in in his barn overalls and with a face and beard like Jesu on the rock in the picture in Oma's front parlour, only Papa had real Power eyes.

And Uncle Walter had a gun, and he took it and loaded his large white shiny teeth one by one out of his laughing mouth into it and pointed it at Papa, and I hollered, sure enough hollered I thought, and woke up. But I guess I hadn't hollered, because Mama didn't come.

And at breakfast Papa said, She's looking *pieserich* again; too many books again, I bet; she don't go outside enough, can't you make her? And Mama said, She's worried for her Uncle Walter maybe; she's awful sensitive, just like me, just like everybody on our side.

Like your Brother Walter, maybe? Papa said. And he wiped the milky coffee wet off his moustache with the back of a hand and didn't take a second cup and went outside.

And pretty soon after that, Uncle Walter got his orders to go overseas, or his part of the army did, and Mama offered for Papa to take his milk cows and keep them so Ruby could go back home to Senlac. And Uncle Walter said, No, never mind about them, Ruby's gonna stay on at the place and she could use the cream cheques. And Mama said, For goodness sake, a hired girl when there's no meals or washing only her own, what kind of sense does *that* make? And Uncle Walter said to never mind about it and maybe Albert wouldn't mind going over every now and then to see how the stove wood and feed chop were holding out. And Mama said Well if that was the case she'd see to that, and Uncle Walter left and all the way to the grid he blew the horn of his Model A with the Union Jack flying bright from its hood ornament.

And Mama told Papa that night about the cows and Papa said phfumpf into his moustache again, but next day he went, even though Uncle Walter wasn't on the ship yet, not even on the train; he was back in the camp in Dundurn.

And Papa came home from over at Uncle Walter's and he said, The bastard. And Mama said, Whatever in the world brought that on? And Papa said, The girl; she's in the family way. And Mama said Oh, and sat down and said, Poor

Walter. And Papa said, Them milk pails full weigh twenty, twenty-five pounds apiece. And Mama said, When? And Papa said, Well as soon as ever they're full, of course, and at least if he'd tooken her to church she'd have his pay and his pension, supposing.

And Mama said quick, A *Katolische*? And from Senlac yet! And Papa said, A *Katolische* can't carry full milk pails no better than anybody else in the family way. And he cleaned himself up and took the coupe down off the blocks — it was faster — and filled her up and cranked her and drove to Dundurn to the army camp.

And in three days time there was the wedding and the pastor never even waited for the health certificate.

And at first Mama and Aunt Emma both said how could they ever make a wedding so quick, but all the women pitched in and cooked too, and fried punschkins and baked strudel and all that. It was a kind of a rule. It wasn't a sin like from the catechism not to help out to cook, but it was a kind of a rule because those who didn't help out cook wouldn't get helped out maybe when it happened to them. They did it on Clara Schumacher one time years ago, Aunt Emma said, and nobody ever forgot.

The homebrew nobody had to make: Old Mr. Bill Knopp always had it hidden in the manure pile. Like, not really in the manure pile, the bottles would get gunked, but in a built pit and the manure put on over the roof real thick and you crawled to it from under his chop bin. Papa knew. Hardly anybody but Papa knew, but if you sat quiet when Old Mr. Bill Knopp and Papa were talking, they didn't bother you if you had in your hand the *Old Greek Myths* or the *Anne of Green Gables*.

And that's about all you needed for a wedding, the pastor and the church were always there and nobody had to make them. And my Aunt Ruby who really wasn't would get made into my real Aunt Ruby and into Mama's sister too; only not really, she was a *Katolische* and from Senlac — but

Mama's sister in the law, they said. And she'd get made too into Uncle Walter's holy wife.

Only she didn't want to.

She didn't want to. They told her how lucky she was, Mama said, and she just got mad and started crying. She had the nerve to say Walter is a bastard, Mama said, as if it don't take two to make a bargain, and she is going to walk to her Uncle Mike's in Prince Albert — walk! can you imagine? Mama said, as soon as ever Walter gives her her wages.

Well he *is* a bastard, Papa said. He'd stopped his ears, I guess, when Mama said the bastard part and he hadn't heard any of the rest, it seemed like. And Mama said, Oh he *is* a bastard, is he? Because he's on *my* side, I suppose; it would never do, I suppose, to remember your own Cousin Bennie. And Papa said, I'll drive her to Prince Albert myself. And Mama said, Stay out of it; the girl says her Uncle Mike is worse than Walter Uhrich even, but at least he has a wife around. And Papa said, She's not as stupid as people say then, good for her. And Mama said, Smart enough to talk; we can't have that; the girl is under sixteen, it turns out. Lucky she has no real folks.

Papa was not much on second-hand talk, so he went over there again, I guess, and talked to my pretty soon Aunt Ruby. And he came back and said, The girl has class; she threw Walter's money at him when he said he'd pay her to marry him.

I guess Papa had tooken Uncle Walter out to the barn for a hour first, to tell him how he'd better bloody well do things.

Well damn it, I want her but she won't, Uncle Walter told him. I asked her first, real proper. I wanted her but she wouldn't have me and sometimes a man can't help himself. And that's when Papa said, Maybe buy her then and I'll help. But it was the wrong thing to try with my Aunt Ruby.

Because Ruby took the money roll that Uncle Walter gave

her and counted out her wages and then threw the rest in the coal pail. And Uncle Walter said, Hey, you little bitch. But he left it there. And then, surprise to Papa, Uncle Walter got down on his knees to Aunt Ruby and cried and told her he wanted to have the baby. Boy or girl, it didn't matter, Uncle Walter said, just don't take the baby away inside her or outside her and he'd promise never to bother her again like that and she could even have a lock on her door to see he kept his promise, only stay.

And Papa said, Think on it please, Ruby; there's a good girl. I'll take the cows and milk them and send you the cream cheques till he comes back; and there'll be me or Abe or Emil here every other day to see are you OK, once Walter's gone.

And Uncle Walter got up off his knees and said, My army cheque would come to you; my army cheque would come to you, remember.

And Ruby went to the window and looked north for quite a long time. And then she went and picked the money out of the coal pail and gave it to Uncle Walter, holding the tens and twenties at the corners with two fingers.

And she said, You're going soon? And Uncle Walter said, Next week. And Ruby said, Go buy a lock and bring along a paper, the farm goes to the baby when you die. Mr. Albert Schroeder will write it out and read it to me on his Bible.

And they did all that, I guess, and then there was the wedding.

The church part was all right, but people didn't bother too much to listen, the pastor was supposed to be good at that part; and anyway it was more important to see how much Aunt Ruby was showing. Sometimes the brides' stomachs stuck out like a pig's bladder blown up to play football on the day of butchering, under their white satin dresses. Aunt Ruby had a stomach that stuck out a little, not much; but it looked kind of funny because she was pretty skinny. She was an awful good looker and pretty skinny, and she never once raised her eyes.

It was after church was the good part. You hardly got to my Opa Uhrich's even in Papa's coupe before the four Old Bill Knopp boys were tuning up the guitar and fiddle in Opa's machine shed. He was neat — so clean and neat you could almost eat off the floor, the women said, in my Opa Uhrich's machine shed.

And Uncle Emil Beckmann and my Cousin Gerda came too, but Auntie Elizabeth stayed home with Floydie, she was still out of commission, Uncle Emil said, since they buried Elsa after she went in to the stallion. And Papa told him to quit talking, it was over; and he went in the coupe and brought them anyway, and Auntie Elizabeth went right away and sat beside Ruby at the bride's table and I got Floydie to hold; he was squirmy and loud but cute and round and rosy.

And while the people danced with a lot of Wha-hoos and foot stomps, except when they were dancing with my new Aunt Ruby, Old Mr. Bill Knopp went around showing his wedding night dolls: the little wooden ones, you held one in each hand and pressed the head with a thumb, flick, I watched under his arm once, and the bride's skirt flew open and there were all her bare parts. And the man, you know what sprung out on him, shame, shame, real red and stiff like Perky's rose when he is sitting on his haunches panting, after chasing the cows too hard in the pasture. And he tried to show Aunt Ruby, Old Mr. Bill Knopp did, his nose white already from the home brew — imagine — and supper hardly over. But Auntie Elizabeth stood up and looked at him in that way she has, not quiet like Papa, but with the Power just aburning. Auntie Elizabeth had the Power eyes; almost always she had the Power eyes. So Old Mr. Bill Knopp went, and never came back again until it was the music for *Schenk die Braut*, and then he put twenty dollars in the dish for my new Aunt Ruby and never even said, How come I can't pin it right on your bosom; in the old days we always did.

And nobody got to kiss the bride, everybody got told so
by Papa. The hand, yes, they could kiss, and Ruby held it
out proper, like a gift to the kisser, with the two big gold
rings on it. Uncle Walter was not cheap. No Uhrich was
ever cheap, even those who were jealous because Opa had
too many half-sections, could never say it. So the people
could dance with the bride, but nobody could kiss her, only
the women.

So after *Schenk die Braut* there was lots more — two days
of it, but I don't know how the people held all the homebrew and potato salad and caraway seed bread, and the
jokes and the dancing and the sausage. I guess my Aunt
Ruby didn't know, either. And when Uncle Walter took her
home on the wedding night, she used the new lock on her
bedroom door and wouldn't come out until he went back to
the army camp; Uncle Walter himself said it.

And when he went overseas it didn't take him too long to
get shot — they liked to send the Canadians to the front
lines; Canadians didn't matter.

And when we heard, Mama couldn't go over to see Aunt
Ruby; she felt too bad; Uncle Walter was, after all, her baby
brother. But it was night-time, so it was better for Papa to
take somebody along to go tell Ruby; people had this way
to talk right away if you went places in the night-time, and
so he took me.

And when Papa told Ruby she said Oh. And she got up
and put the baby in his cradle and sat down beside him and
rocked the cradle a little bit with one toe. And she did that
for quite a while and nobody said any more and I wondered
if she was sleeping. But then she got done doing that and
she got up and held out her hand to Papa. Maybe you'd bring me them cows back home tomorrow, Mr. Albert
Schroeder, she said; I better be milking them myself — you
been too good already — now that I can take Percy along
with me to the barn.

HOW COME A ANGEL COULD EVER BE CALLED A SWAN?

When Papa used to come to me and say, Why don't you go to Mama, she's crying again, I didn't know what to do or to say but I went, I was supposed to. When your Mama is a crier you know it pretty early and soon it doesn't mean much. But when your Papa cries that's really something hard to see. When your only Papa in all the world ever cries, it's a hard one. I never saw my Papa cry, only once, and for me, it was enough. Papa was never a crier.

Germans aren't. Germans aren't criers, anyhow; it isn't allowed, except for maybe a few, like Mama. It isn't so much the Bible says not, because Jesu, he did it. I wondered to myself when the pastor read it: And Jesu wept. A man. Imagine. Jesu wept, it said there, so I asked Papa, I didn't want to believe it. And Papa said, Ya sure, a man has a right to cry sometimes. But till Papa said it and did it, I never ever believed a man would cry.

It didn't have to do with my Auntie Elizabeth though. You're always mooning about that woman, Mama used to tell Papa, but the time Papa cried didn't have anything to do with my Auntie Elizabeth.

Anyway, Papa wasn't mooning; he was studying in the

encyclopedia, he told me so, and he had his pipe in one
hand and a finger caught to save his place in the page about
hydroelectricity, he showed me when I asked. Hydro means
to do with water. Why can't they just call it water electri-
city? I said to Papa, and he said Hmmm? And Mama said,
Quit thinking about her; she made her bed, now let her lie
in it; you're always mooning about that Elizabeth Beckmann, she's too fancy, she thinks, to be called Lizzie, well
let her be fancy enough to put up with him; if she treated
him better, you know where, he wouldn't have to be running always to see that Elmyra Bitner.

And so that was Uncle Emil. Uncle Emil Beckmann.
Uncle Emil with the gold, gold hair and the white teeth, the
teeth so white it was like the white leg rings you put on the
chickens; only the chicken rings, they didn't stay white, but
Uncle Emil Beckmann's teeth, they did. He smiled with
them a lot. When he was at church or at a C.C.F. meeting or
running for the schoolboard, Uncle Emil Beckmann smiled
with his teeth a lot. He never got smile crinkles around his
mouth or eyes or anything, but his teeth, they really could
smile a lot.

He had a white stallion too. I don't know why but Uncle
Emil Beckmann always had to have a white stallion. The
first one his mama bought for him. I never knew her; nobody around ever knew her. Uncle Emil Beckmann came
riding one day from Swan River, Manitoba on his snow
white stallion with the rolling eyes, and he took up land and
nobody knew his mama or anybody else called Beckmann
until he made Auntie Elizabeth one and then she birthed
some more of them, that was Elsa and Gerda and Floydie. I
could say Floydie-Two and Murray, too, but what's the
sense, they don't belong in it, they weren't even born yet.

Auntie Elizabeth bought Uncle Emil the second white
stallion. I heard Grampa Schroeder tell Papa. Grampa
Schroeder swore; it was in our barn and Grampa Schroeder
swore and called Uncle Emil Beckmann that fuckin bastard

and Papa said, For sure, for sure. And then I came out from my horse Sermon's stall to hear more and Papa said, Say, how about you go on up to the henhouse and see if you can find maybe six new eggs; I betcha Mama might want to make a angel food yet for supper. And so I had to go, but I knew aleady Auntie Elizabeth paid for the second white stallion with the cows Grampa gave her when she up and married Uncle Emil instead of going back to Normal School to learn to be a teacher. I knew because Gerda told me once.

And so it wasn't about the white stallion Papa cried, either, but it somehow had something to do with it. I can't remember just exactly how it all went, but the white stallion had something to do with it.

Oh yes, I do so remember. It was like this. It was, the stallion was white, but Elsa was white, too. Only she was white like a angel, and loved Uncle Emil too much; he was a man who didn't stay home much. And it was the night of the church Christmas concert. You have to tell a little bit about the church Christmas concert, too, but partly because it is nice to tell it.

The church Christmas concert was always glory. I mean, it was the shining glory of God and Jesu always that night, and everybody knew it. Nobody was supposed to think about presents or *Jingle Bells* or candy bags like at the school Christmas concert. Well now, yes, candy bags there were; it was allowed; but not allowed were presents and Santa Claus and *Jingle Bells, Jingle Bells*. They weren't holy. Well, the candy maybe. If it was at a holy church Christmas concert it was likely holy, or else Germans wouldn't do that.

You would leave home for the church Christmas concert right after supper and already it was dark. You would have the cows milked and fed, Papa and you; and he would tell you to throw Sermon a extra oat bundle; it was Christmas Eve and if you came out to see him at midnight, he'd be on his knees saying thank you to Jesu for the clean straw and the oat bundle and the warm dry barn. And I said, Papa, *you* were the one hauled in the straw and cut the oats; don't you care if Sermon does that? And Papa said, No, I don't think so; I kind of thank Him too for a strong back and big hands so I can do all that.

So that was good and all right. And you would carry the lantern for Papa, not the gasoline one with the big white eye; the gasoline one hissed and got so hot it burned your legs sometimes when you carried it. Mostly you carried the coal oil one, the nice yellow one; our coal oil lantern never smoked its chimney window all black, Papa knew how to keep the wick trimmed. At Uncle Emil Beckmann's, Auntie Elizabeth cleaned the lantern chimneys and trimmed the wicks, but at our place Papa always did that.

And you'd go in the house after that and Mama had the borscht already in the soup plates and the tub for baths out and the copper boiler steaming, because believe you her, nobody went to the church Christmas concert from our place smelling of cow barn, we might as well put our minds to that.

And I always had a new dress. Mama made it. And my Cousin Gerda, she was the size of me, she always got one too, and so did my Cousin Elsa, she was bigger, a little bit, but it was mostly neck. My Cousin Elsa, she had the Schroeder neck like her mama, Auntie Elizabeth. Mama said so. Mama wasn't a Schroeder and so, thank goodness, she didn't have the Schroeder neck.

But Elsa looked beautiful anyway. Elsa always looked beautiful. She was sort of like Uncle Emil in a way; Uncle Emil was all white and gold, and Elsa was all white and white. Everything seemed white about her. Her hair was the whitest thing. It was white when she was geboren a baby and it just got whiter and whiter, and so did her arms and legs and teeth and, somehow, even her eyes.

You know what? Elsa is like a angel and beautiful, I said

to Papa going to the church Christmas concert that night. It was already dark and we and the cutter and the horses were cutting crisp-crunch, crispa-crispa crunch over the hard-packed road to church. And the stars were out, no moon, and Papa was watching them again, he had this habit of doing that.

And Papa said, only more like to the stars, not to me: She is a swan and enchanted, and she hurts my heart to see her.

And Mama said, What a thing to say. And in front of this one, too; she thinks too much as it is, it isn't healthy.

And I said, Is, too! Mostly when you were going out someplace you could do that; other times you better not say to Mama, Is, too! And then we were at the church and so was everybody else. And women and kids went in right away — Germans don't be late for anything — whilst the men put the horses away in the big long barn and smoked a last smoke before they took a sprinkle of sensen behind the lip and came in, too, smoothing down their hair with one hand, those who'd forgot their comb again.

And in the church it was beautiful, beautiful with the glory; not just like Sunday night church in summer for the missions in Africa when it was hot and your bloomers always stuck with you to the seat when you were supposed to stand up to pray. The night of the holy church concert there were only candles in the church. Candles, candles, candles, all over the place: in the windows, on the altar, in the big round candelabra hanging from the ceiling. The candelabra swung and made shadows when Uncle Abe Schroeder took his long candle lighter, it was red velvet and had gold tassels, and reached up — he had to stand on his toes, yet he was a big man — and lit the twelve white candles and made more glory for the night of the church Christmas concert.

The candles were as white as Uncle Emil Beckmann's teeth and Elsa's. They were glowing white. They glowed with whiteness. It was very nice.

And then came the concert.

And the whole Sunday School and the whole Young People's Luther League sang *Komm' Herr Jesu, Jesu Schön*; they sang it in four parts; it made you feel real good; it started the glory. And nobody preached, it spoiled the glory, but everybody in the Sunday School, even the littlest ones, said a piece in German.

German was beautiful. To speak a piece in German was glory, too, like the singing, for the words made soft music on the tongue before they even got out of your mouth. To speak German was more than glory; it was beautiful.

And then my Cousin Elsa came to speak her piece, and here if she wasn't a angel, really a angel, dressed all in white and with wings, even — she'd sewed it all herself. I couldn't. Gerda, my Cousin Gerda couldn't either; we always pricked our fingers with the needle whenever we tried.

And I knew Elsa was going to speak a piece like a angel, and I wanted to watch for her to come out, but all at once, just all of a sudden, she was there by the manger. Like magic out of nowhere she was there like a angel on the first glory night, and she spoke her German piece loud and clear. And she was a wounded angel because one of her wings drooped. And I felt the glory of a wounded angel made whole again to speak to the Jesu in his holy manger, and the glory got inside me, inside my very throat, so warm and golden I opened up my mouth just a little and I said, Oh thank you, Jesu.

It would have been better in German. I thought later it would have been more glory to say the thank you in German, but somehow just then for the wonder of it, I somehow forgot.

And Elsa and that church Christmas concert were just so beautiful I carried them home inside.

And the next day when I got up Mama said Papa had gone over to Uncle Emil Beckmann's. And when he got home he had tears standing there in his eyes.

Mama said, You mean even on Christmas Eve? He had to go after Church Concert to see Elmyra Bitner?

And Papa said, Yes. Yes, yes, yes, Papa said, talking to his big two hands. And the Little Swan, she always saw too much; always.

Then all at once I got goose pimple chills, and I stood and listened, just outside the kitchen door, until I knew what they meant. They'd found Elsa in with the stallion. She'd taken the key against all orders and after midnight Uncle Emil came home and found her in with the stallion, found her on the floor of the big box-stall and over her Uncle Emil's wild white stallion bought him by Auntie Elizabeth's cow money.

I went into the kitchen then. And there was Papa standing with tears in his eyes. And I couldn't stand it. I went to Papa and pulled at his sleeve and he bent down to me.

Papa, I said, Elsa maybe took the key but I don't think she was a bad girl. You know what? I bet she went, a angel, and took the key against all orders so that she could see the stallion on his knees at midnight giving thanks to the new holy Lord.

And I never forgot how my Papa put his head in his hands then, and cried.

I don't know what's the matter with boys that they have to act so stupid all the time. When you're in grade five and boys start acting stupid and bringing you chocolate bars to school, and you know their pas always bring out only one apiece for their kids on Saturdays from town and every one costs a whole nickel, then you know the boys are starting to act stupid and it's a real pain.

Whenever they start saying on the ball diamond, It's OK, it's OK, instead of Why dincha catch it, Stoopid, you know they're starting to get stupid themselves in that other way. And when your friend Albertina, who is two years older and your best friend in all the world, seems to think it's OK for them to do that, well what can you do about it? You have to stop and think about it, even if it makes you go Yukk.

It starts on Valentine's Day. The stupidness always seems to start on Valentine's Day. With putting L O V E on valentine cards even for boys because Miss Myse for four years and now Elda Schwartz says yes you have to give to boys.

First we had Miss Myse in School and now we have Elda

Schwartz. We have to call her Miss Schwartz now, even if she used to be Elda Schwartz who used to give you a good klatsch over the ear if you didn't know your Bible verse in Saturday School where your folks sent you all summer to store up enough God to get you through the winter when the roads were bad and you lived seven miles from church. She used to be Elda Schwartz but now she is through Normal School and her pa is on the Blenheim schoolboard, so she is not a scared one and still pretty good at klatsching you over the ear — don't ever tell; your mother will just say you had it coming and maybe Papa should give you a couple little whacks each hand so you'll remember to watch yourself better for a while.

On Valentine's Day, never mind how old you were, you had to make valentines. One for every darnbody in the school. It didn't matter if you didn't like them, it was a rule. If somebody got 37 valentines and there were 39 people in school — don't count the teacher; teacher is a different thing — you might do a psychological damage to somebody inside their heads and that wasn't allowed anymore.

Elda Schwartz used to be crazy about Miss Myse, who had started it all, and Miss Schwartz had got Psychology in Normal School. Elda Schwartz, besides, remembered the time before Miss Myse, when somebody had done a psychological damage to *her* inside the head, that being one of the big boys giving a store-bought valentine to six other girls and none at all to Elda Schwartz who really loved him.

Miss Schwartz said *love* like it was just another word, like work or even cow, and wasn't hard to say at all. But you could kind of remember Elda Schwartz telling you in Saturday School that God liked you and you had better like him back; you could remember Mrs. Pastor catching her out on it and saying, Oh but Elda, liebe, many of us He does not *like* at all, we are such sinners, but oh how He does *love* us; you could remember Elda Schwartz then getting red as high up as her chin, it was a pretty big one, but not letting the red come up any farther. When you want to be a teacher you have to be strict with yourself.

But Elda Schwartz then had one year of Miss Myse and after that she went away to Normal School where they gave you Psychology, and now she could give this Object Lesson From Real Life and say love out loud any time she wanted. And when she told about the psychological damage part, Miss Schwartz smirked a little, because she told it whilst fondling a shiny diamond ring (my friend Albertina Bitner had already heard it was glass) on her engagement ring finger. Because the upshot of the Object Lesson was that the big boy who had not given her a valentine that time was the one — surprise, surprise — who *had* given her the new shiny diamond glass ring.

This big boy had loved her desperately back then, Miss Schwartz said, but was honestly and truly afraid to say it, and even though he got shyly around to it a few years later, at the time he had unknowingly done a psychological damage inside Miss Schwartz's head, and so now it was her sacred mission to see it didn't happen to the young souls she was in charge of here in Blenheim School.

One had an obligation, Miss Schwartz said, to be the best example one could during one's years in God's green and pleasant land. She had a churchy way of putting things, Miss Schwartz did. It came, my friend Albertina said, from being too many years in charge of klatsching people over the ears in Saturday School when people wouldn't listen or hadn't got their memory verses right.

So anyway, we had to make these stupid valentines. Forty-three that year. One good thing at least: you didn't have to make for the teacher. For the teacher it was allowed to get a store-bought one, if you could afford it. Mama always got me two. I asked her. She said, You're foolish; it doesn't pay, you know. But she did it, and I traded one, it didn't matter which, to my friend Albertina for the chance to drive Jack, the Bitners' spry new cart pony, to our gate every day after school.

Only Albertina went to school now from the Bitners. Zenina was done and the little roly-poly boys with black curls weren't ready yet. But Albertina still drove the cart, instead of riding. Sometimes in the ditch you might find beer bottles and anyway, she liked to give rides; anybody could come with if you hadn't called her for the last week even once a Stinker.

Brian Montgomery was good at it. I thought it was because he was English and his mother acted like him and his big brother Eddie were lords or dukes or kings or something. Germans liked all those things too, but only if they acted like lords or dukes or kings ought to — a little bit better and sensibler and royaler than anybody else, royaler than the pastor or the doctor in town and better than anybody else in the whole world except maybe Jesu. But the Montgomerys never went to church and so maybe that's why Mrs. Montgomery only knew the nose in the air part about being royal.

Brian Montgomery didn't like me or Albertina Bitner much, but he lived a half-a-mile further from school than even the Bitners. And Eddie Montgomery couldn't spare a horse that year during spring seeding for his brother to ride to school, so he had to walk to the Bitners' place and hitch a ride with Albertina. Eddie gave him twenty-five cents to go and ask, only not tell their mother — it was bad enough Eddie went there sometimes late at night to talk C.C.F. with Mrs. Elmyra Bitner.

So I was driving Albertina's spry new cart pony, Jack, then, and Albertina got me to let Brian Montgomery drive him, instead. Brian Montgomery really wanted to. To ride a old work plug to school is one thing, but to drive a two-year-old with stand-up ears, that is another thing and that is for sure.

I didn't want to let him drive but Albertina said, What the heck, let him see how bad he is. So I did. But he got so good so fast, he got cocky and wanted the whole time to make the pony gallop.

So Albertina finally said, Nuts to that, give the lines over to Alvena. And Brian Montgomery said, Nah, I wanna take him the rest of the way. Let me. Come on. I'll go slow, I promise.

And he gave the lines a sneaky little flip on the pony's twitchy rump whilst looking Albertina straight in the eye and smiling in that Montgomery way, sincere, sincere, and saying that he wouldn't.

But Albertina said, Fair is fair; you give the lines over to Alvena. And he yanked on them, his lip stuck out just for all the world like a Montgomery, and the cart pony rared a little and blew snorts out of his nose to show he didn't like it — he was young and had to have a sharp bit yet.

And Albertina grabbed the lines and said, Give here; don't you ever do that again. And Brian Montgomery said, You Stinker. Stinker, Stinker, Stinker. And he leapt off the cart into the dust of the road and fell and hurt his knee, but pretended he didn't.

And Albertina stopped the cart and looked back and saw where his breeches had got split open; they were khaki, no, worse — light as a turkey egg almost, but with no spots. And so Albertina saw the blood on them and said, Come on, Montgomery, you can drive again at Sandhill Corner.

But Brian Montgomery hollered, Stinker! Go suck eggs! I don't need you or your stupid old rattle trap or your stupid old crowbait, and your old man's sitting in The Pen in Prince Albert, he killed a crazy woman.

And Albertina got red and flicked the lines just a little and whistled quite low and quite short just once between her teeth and off set the cart pony, making dust, and with Brian Montgomery hollering Stinker, Dirty Old Stinker, after us down the road. To call somebody Stinker was worse, just about, than to talk dirt about somebody's pa, because Stinker meant you wore barn overalls to school, the ones you milked in, and you never cleaned the manure off your boots before you came.

So from then on, Eddie Montgomery got on the field late because he had to bring Brian to school. But he got tired of it and started going to horse sales to make sure he'd have a spare horse or two by next spring when the land work came on. Eddie wound up, early winter, with two green-broke broncos he wanted tired out real good by spring, so he put real hefty control bits on the pair and turned Brian loose with them. Of course Brian Montgomery dashed and pranced the pair, keeping their heads high, too high; keeping their heads high and straining like old-time carriage horses in picture books. Brian pranced them straining until it snowed enough and got cold enough to use the closed-in caboose.

A closed-in caboose is a scare for new horses. It stinks of fire to them, Papa said, and scares them silly. To carry a something behind you with smoke smells and sparks coming out of it, is a scare for new horses.

They upset him the first day just outside the Bitners' front gate. Albertina said Brian was slapping those broncos across the rear end like he was on a race track and it was worth a half a million dollars to rare a little every hundred steps. To get a horse to rare up on his hind legs like a circus horse was something the Montgomerys seemed to fancy.

Eddie Montgomery — Mama said he was dependable — was only ten years older than Brian, but he farmed the Montgomery farm himself. His pa had gone back to the old country to get made into a soldier; he didn't even bother to wait until there was a war. Eddie Montgomery was just the same as Brian about raring a horse — Mama didn't know it — and he even wore spurs sometimes, it made you laugh, and he wore leather patches on his tweed jacket, even if he'd just bought it brand new yesterday from a store. He called his mother *mater* once. I asked Papa about it. Papa said it was the old English way for the rich and the royal ones; they used to talk the Latin in the old days, like maybe around the time of King Arthur. And so I guess "mater" is all right.

I guess there wasn't too much wrong with *Brian* Montgomery, except he slapped horses and made them rare up, and he called you Stinker whenever he got mad.

And so he upset the caboose, and so Albertina and Zenina and Sabrina and Mrs. Elmyra Bitner helped him get it right side up again. Ernestina didn't. Ernestina went and got married as soon as ever Zenina was done school, and so she wasn't there, or else she would have helped to do it.

And Mrs. Bitner said lucky he had no fire in the heater, he coulda burn hisself; it woulda spread hot coals from here to hell the way them broncos drug that caboose over one snowbank and another until they got it mired.

And Mrs. Bitner said, How would it be to take turns with our rig; Albertina has to go anyway. But Brian wouldn't. To not show up at school with the new broncos would make a lot of questions. He was white, though, white as could be, and he said how about Albertina driving *his* team, he guessed he'd hurt his elbow.

And his elbow stayed hurt all winter, except when he was wrestling in the snow with somebody who had called him Stinker, or throwing snowballs with ice chunks inside them at the girls at noon hours.

And so my friend Albertina drove the Montgomery horses the rest of that winter and liked it.

And all that winter, whenever I said Brian Montgomery stunk, stunk right out loud for throwing snowballs with ice chunks in them, Albertina said, Oh he doesn't mean nothing; the others make them, so he has to too. Brian Montgomery is gonna be a big league ball pitcher and he can throw so close he could hit the eye of a cat on the run, just like Menno Friesen on the Mennonite ball team.

And I said so what, he still stunk. But any time I said anything at all, my friend Albertina Bitner said Brian Montgomery was this and that and the other thing — all *good*. All of a sudden, so far as my friend Albertina seemed to be concerned, Brian Montgomery would not say Stinker if he got shot twice by a skunk.

And right after school Brian would call, Come on Bert, let's get the old nags on the road. It was smart, he thought, to call new broncos nags and do them a favour and get them on the road.

And they'd go off together to the barn, pushing each other into the snow and making angels in the ball diamond when there was a new fall of snow and we came out after school to what Miss Schwartz called a Virgin Uncharted Expanse Fit For Adventurous Explorers, almost making the capital letters with her new-teacher eyes.

And I would not go with them. I would stand on the doorstep and wait for Papa to come and get me. Mama would not let me drive in anybody else's closed-in caboose; she said they were too dangerous.

Well, anyway, came the Valentine's Day party. And at the Valentine's Day party when everybody else got forty-two homemade valentines and Miss Schwartz was supposed to get forty-three store-bought ones, Brian Montgomery gave Miss Schwartz one cut out of a red Christie Cracker box and Albertina one that cost twenty-five cents all by itself and had a fancy name on the bottom back and came from Eaton's and not from the Fifteen Cent Store.

And I followed them out to the barn after to ask Albertina how she liked the poem I wrote for her valentine. It was a good poem, TO A SPECIAL FRIEND, and I even cried a little when I wrote it and twice more whilst I printed it in red ink on the pure white heart I cut from Mama's Snow Vellum writing tablet.

So I went out to the barn.

And Brian Montgomery had his arm around Albertina.

And I went and told Miss Schwartz.

And Miss Schwartz pressed her lips together tight and

sighed a little. And then she said, Alvena dear, why not take off your things until your father comes and let's see if there's any hot cocoa left from the party. And there was, and we drank it whilst waiting for Papa, and she told me the poem I wrote to put inside her store-bought valentine was as beautiful as anything by E. Pauline Johnson.

And she got me to read it out loud when we finished our cocoa, and then we admired all her valentines and all of mine, and I was just trying on her new shiny diamond engagement ring on my engagement ring finger when we heard the brass bells on Papa's cutter.

And he was calling Hoo-hoo for me before I even got my overshoes buckled and Miss Schwartz had wrapped my new red crocheted scarf from Oma Schroeder good and snug and warm about my ears.

When my friend Albertina Bitner had a birthday, she never asked anybody else to it but me.

She asked Brian Montgomery once, I guess, and he wouldn't go. That wasn't this time; it was another time. It was the birthday after she drove Brian Montgomery's new green-broke broncos to school for him. After he upset in the closed-in caboose one time, and it scared him. He wouldn't admit, but it scared him. And so he drove the road between Montgomery's and Bitner's with his broncos all winter, forty below no matter, in the open cutter — the fancy one, all paint and varnish and even a green leather seat, you had to wonder how they made it green, that leather; and right away your mind got acting smart aleck and told you they sure as heck never got it that colour off a cow.

The mind was a funny thing. Miss Schwartz in school talked lots about the mind; she'd had a course in it in Normal School. About The Original Mind and about The Conditioned Mind. She put capital letters on them when she put them on the board for the big girls taking Correspondence. She didn't have to teach the people taking Correspondence, she only had to correct things they did. But she

did it anyway. She taught and taught them. It seemed to
take a lot of speaking to do it. And she put capital letters on
a lot of things; she even put capital letters on things when
she just spoke about them, never mind when she put them
on the board. It doesn't matter that she did it; it's only
funny how she could seem to somehow do that so plain.

I didn't understand about The Original Mind or The
Conditioned Mind, but I liked those words a lot. And a
funny thing, once Miss Schwartz talked about them and
talked about them one morning — I should have been doing
arithmetic, but I was somehow listening and getting tired of
both of those minds, she told too much about them — when
all at once, bingo, a funny thing, it was like *I* had the both
of those minds right there inside me — only maybe it
wasn't inside me; it was maybe all around me, circling in a
Jesu ring of light all around the head, circling like the bees
in the grade three Reader circling the head of the man with
the bonnet and the bees sat upon it — there was a picture
there with the words on the same page of the Reader and I
never forgot it.

The mind was sure a funny thing. Because after Miss
Schwartz talked and talked about the two minds it was like
I had them; and sometimes one of them would talk to me,
and sometimes it was like I wasn't there at all and it was
two other people talking about me in — or maybe all
around — my own head.

"She wants to go to that party," one part said once, said
once in the morning early; I'd just wakened up and hadn't
even said the *Komm Herr Jesu* yet.

"She'll go," the other part said. It said it further away,
somehow. Overtop the other talking part, or maybe on the
other side of it. It was like hearing somebody talk on the
crystal set radio from Hong Kong or from Radio City
Music Hall over at Uncle Emil Schroeder's on winter
nights — you had to take turns listening if there were cousins there, but if only you and Mama and Papa went, you

could sit and listen a long time. Sometimes it tickled the ears.

So when the crystal set radio voice said into my head, or around it, She wants to go: She'll go, I jumped right out of bed, I thought maybe it was Papa and Mama, just getting up out of bed and talking; they sometimes did that. Only when I went to see, there was nobody in their room; they were already gone from it. And so I went barefeet downstairs to the kitchen; the stair steps felt good, cool and clean and good, hardly ever did you get any sharp dirt junk on your feet from Mama's stairstep linoleum.

Nobody was in the kitchen, either. I said quick, then, the *Komm Herr Jesu*; it was as though maybe if I'd said it like you are supposed to, before coming down the stairs, then maybe I would have found Papa and Mama in the kitchen and saying I could go.

So I went back upstairs to put clothes on, and I said a whole bunch of *Komm Herr Jesu* and *Bitte, Herr Jesu*; and I wouldn't let my mind say party, party, party at all. I wouldn't even let it make the pictures of the Bitners' big kitchen and everybody in there talking and laughing.

I put on a clean shirt and overalls, and school socks. And going downstairs again I felt hot already, but the walls felt nice, felt clean cool on the hands; you had to hang on a little to the walls — even if just touch, touch, touch — going down Mama's linoleum steps if you had slippy school socks on.

In the kitchen everything was sun. There was even the smell of sun, only it was really the coal oil stove, the flame turned real low, just enough to keep the double boiler hot where the Sonny Boy Cereal was getting ready; when you lifted the lid, the steam steamed out first and smelled good even without the cream and sugar. And once the steam was out, you could see the Sonny Boy Cereal in the pot, kind of shiny on top and with the dark black seedy bits in it, the ones that were real slidey if you tried to catch one between the front teeth and bit it apart because when you did, it tasted a little of butter.

Only this day I didn't stop to look at it or smell it. I just went right through to the back porch and found my barn shoes and I went out to the cow barn. The sun was hot already on the head, Mama would say, For pity sake now, where's your sun hat in this heat?

Inside the cow barn it was dark at first; cool and dark. It felt good all over you, all at once; it gave you a shiver that wasn't really a shiver. It was like you were just out of the bath tub, summers in the kitchen, with the window shades pulled against the heat and your towel wet because it fell in the tub and so you weren't dried off yet.

The cow barn smelled of clean cows and milk. Our cows hardly ever got a chance to manure up the barn; Mama would get up from the milk stool and go and carry it right out, or tell Papa. She said why should a person smell manure a whole hour twice a day all their life — it made you smell manure then whenever you poured milk into a cake batter or into a pitcher for the morning's porridge.

So Mama and Papa, in the cow barn, they both did that. Carried the manure out.

I stopped first in the empty calf stall and checked for the three white snowball kittens my friend Albertina Bitner and I had got from over at Louie and Francine Hoffer's. And they were there, all three of them, lip-lapping warm white milk out of a bowl. Papa never forgot; he gave them the first squirts from the first cow. He just got right up again when he had enough for one bowl and went and fed the three white snowball kittens. So they were getting as round as real snowballs now, because Papa never forgot.

So, funny thing, the words and the pictures about my friend Albertina's birthday party stopped; they stopped just like that; they sort of melted into nothing. And then for a while there was nothing there, just the real picture, there on the floor of the calf stall, of the three white snowball kit-

tens squatting lap-lap-lap in a circle around the blue porridge bowl I'd snicked for them from the kitchen cupboard
and then told Mama, when she asked, it had a little crack in
it.

The three white kittens were three white round snowballs and the blue porridge bowl was a round blue sky. It
had no business in the floor of the calf pen. The milk inside
it was as white as a kitten or a vanilla ice cream cone at the
Chinaman's in town, or like a cloud. The three white kittens were lapping a white kitten ice cream cone cloud.
They were lapping it with soft pink tiny tongues, lap-lap-
lap-lap-lap.

And while I watched, the feeling came. It was like the
feeling that came walking with Papa and the morning sun
beside the mint slough when you were little. It was like the
feeling that came the first time you saw Aunt Ruby
Uhrich's Percy, pink and roly-poly clean after his bath,
kicking in his cradle in the sun, with little magic golden
specks dancing in the sunbeams right from the top of the
kitchen window to Percy lying there getting blessed, only
with no angels flying around like in the picture in Oma
Uhrich's Bible where the God sunshine shone on the Baby
Lord God Jesu in the stable in gold-specked streams too,
just like it did in Aunt Ruby Uhrich's kitchen on her pink
round Percy bare naked and cute in his cradle.

It was the same feeling in the calf pen with the three
white kittens. It started in your head, sort of; way up in the
head like when you took a good big smell of the mint
slough, and it sort of blew apart in there, only soft, like a
goosefeather pillow that falls apart, no reason; and it sort of
fell down and around and all over you and all through you,
like a good warm rain out in the pasture with Papa beside
you saying, "Well now, won't this make the hay and the little girls grow?"

Then, all at once, into the feeling, with you squatted like
a kitten watching the three white snowball kittens in the

calf pen, there came Mama's voice saying, "Well to let her go there after school for supper is one thing, but to let her sleep overnight there? Well of course it wouldn't be *you* would have to clean up the bedbugs and the lice."

And right away you came Bang! out of the feeling, and a part of you wanted to run right to where Mama and Papa were milking, but another part of you, a bossy part of you, almost as clear as the crystal set radio, hollered to you, SIT!

And so you sat, and heard the slip, slip-strip of the milk streaming out of the cows' bags and into the milk pails, and you heard the cows breathing big and in rhythm, and you heard one of them belch, big, but easy, like she didn't really mean to do it; and you even heard the soft lip-lip-lip of the kittens' tongues taking up the last of the milk.

And after you had heard all of that, you heard Papa say, "Well now, I don't know about that. Elmyra Bitner may be a lot of things, but one thing she isn't, is afraid of hard work. You been there yourself a time or two, haven't you, quilting for the church missions and like that? Now do you really think Elmyra Bitner would put up with bedbugs or lice?"

"I suppose *you've* been there a time or two quilting for the church missions," Mama said. "Maybe you've been *more* than a time or two at Elmyra Bitner's, nights."

Papa laughed. "*You* know where I've been, nights," Papa said. "And you know it wouldn't hurt to let Alvena go; you know it would do her a worlda good, and so would it that nice young Albertina Bitner. It's not many'll spare the time to take their kids and fetch them home in haying season, you know that."

"There's not *any*," Mama said. "There's not any woman gonna let her kids go to a party at Elmyra Bitner's, and I bet you just any money you want on that."

"Well then," Papa said. "Couldn't you let her go, then? Don't you think you could just show up all them fine Christian women and let our Alvena go?"

Right then I knew Mama would. I knew it so sure I jumped up and ran to where they were milking so fast that Mama looked up to see what was the commotion even while she was saying, "Oh well, all right, all right then; I guess she can go." Then she looked at me a little sharper, there wasn't much light in the cow barn.

"For pity sake now," she said, "where's your sun hat in this heat?"

So then that very day after school, Mama looked through all the Christmas and birthday presents in the big blue trunk where she kept things she got on Christmas and on birthdays and said, "Oh for pity sake!" when she unwrapped them. And in the trunk she found a red flat thin square box with four embroidered hankies folded to make sort of petals in the four corners, and another one folded to sort of make the centre part of a square hankie flower. They were pretty and I liked them, but Mama said that even for a woman they were not big enough for even one good blow.

I wished she'd let me give Albertina two big red polka-dot hankies, new, like Papa always had in his outside overalls. And Mama argued a little. She said it wasn't dainty for a girl to have them and why encourage such things anyway. But finally she let me, so I wrapped them up in tissue paper and I wrote Albertina a On Your Birthday poem to go with them.

The next day I got to wear a party dress to school; it was white organdy with pink roses all over it; I liked it; and I had Albertina's present in my school bag; it was wrapped up nice — the red bandana hankies and the box of little hankies and the poem — in saved-up birthday present paper. Mama ironed the paper for me nice and smooth; it hardly

showed a wrinkle, and she showed me how to cut off the
bad edges after you drew a line, straight, on the paper with
a ruler.

When Albertina picked me up at the gate the next day,
she told me I looked swell in my pink-roses party dress. She
was wearing overalls, just like every day.

And the girls in school said, "Where you going all
dressed up?" but all I said was, "I'm going to supper; any
law against that?" If you talked smart they sometimes let
you alone.

"To Bitners', I suppose," somebody said.

"Big potatoes!" somebody said.

And right then I almost said about the birthday party, but
I didn't, Albertina shook her head at me, Don't.

And so nobody asked Albertina what she got for her
birthday, and nobody royal bumped her; grabbed her legs
and arms and whooshed her high in the air as they could
and then bounced her down, sometimes hard, sometimes
too hard, if somebody let go a leg or a arm where the
ground was hard in the schoolyard.

It hurt too much on the hinder when they did that; Albertina said so. And so I never said I was going to her house for
a birthday; it was hard not to, but I never did.

And when we got to Albertina's place and put Jack out in
the corral with some oats and water underneath a shade
tree, we went in the house, first giving a whoosh of the
hand to get the flies off the screen door.

The kitchen was full of bread smells. There were loaves
of bread all over. In the kitchen was Zenina and the three
little black-haired boys. And Zenina said, "Oh. Home already?" She was putting more bread in the oven. It was hot
in the kitchen. Her face looked all hot, too. Her long hair
hung over her face and mostly hid it. What you could see of
it was red and hot.

The three little boys stood in a circle around her. They
were watching her put the bread in the oven. Anyway, they

were watching her when we came in. But when we were in they looked over to Albertina and me; all three of them looked at the same time, like it was one head and eyes they had and not three of them, and then they went back to watching Zenina put the bread in the oven.

Albertina crinkled up her nose. She took a good whiff of the bread smell. She said, "I guess it came out sour on you again."

"I don't know what more to do about it," Zenina said, holding one of the little boys back with one hand because he'd had his head almost inside the oven, watching the bread go in. She put the last load in and shut the door and stuck an old butcher knife up it to hold it shut; when the spring goes in the oven door you have to know enough to do that.

Then she bent and looked at the oven thermometer, holding another little boy out of her way to do that, and put a stick of wood in the stove. The wood was fetched by the first little boy, who ran quick to the wood box and got it as soon as ever Zenina put her hand on the lid lifter to look did the fire need more wood for the baking.

"Sour, sour. It makes you tired. It's like it's got stuck in the pans or the yeast or the flour or something. I just don't know what more to do about it anymore," Zenina said.

"Aw, what the hell," Albertina said. "We'll just put more jam on it."

"No store bread left," Zenina said, taking the butcher knife out of the oven door and peeking inside the oven. "Visitor for supper too."

"Oh," Albertina said. "Did it have to be tonight, for Chrisake?"

"Language!" Zenina said.

And I thought it was a funny thing, what Albertina said, I had her present along and everything and she had asked me. And I was going to ask her, as soon as we got alone again, only somebody said then, outside the door, "...

bloody hoppers, twenny-seven to the blade that year," and
the screen door opened and in came Mrs. Bitner and Uncle
Emil Beckmann and a few flies.

"Hallo, hallo, hallo," Mrs. Bitner said. Nobody much
said hello when you came to the Bitners' place, but Mrs.
Bitner, she said enough for everybody. Mrs. Bitner came
right up to me and put out her hand. "Long time no see,
Miss Alvena Schroeder," she said. "And how's everybody
over at your place? How's your papa and mama keeping
anyway?"

"Good," I said. "Pretty good."

"That's good," Mrs. Bitner said. She let go my hand
then. I was glad. She was a hard shaker and a long one. She
had overalls on and field boots, men's, and a hat that used
to be Mr. Bitner's Sunday one before he got sent to Prince
Albert; maybe she thought no use to save it if she had to
buy a new field hat for herself.

Mrs. Bitner's face was all over field dirt. The only part
that wasn't was where the sweat had run down in little
streaks from underneath Mr. Bitner's once Sunday hat.

Her hand was all over field dirt too. She wiped it down
her overalls before she shook, only the overalls were all over
field dirt, the same as her hand, so the hand was still pretty
gunky when we shook.

I wanted to wipe my hand off, after, but I didn't want to
do it on my party dress; so instead I wiped my two hands
together, sort of to spread around the field dirt. Only I
didn't do it until later. I didn't want her to see me do that.

"And I don't suppose you know *this* man at all?" Mrs.
Bitner said, taking Uncle Emil Beckmann by the elbow
from where he was standing quiet by the wall right next to
the kitchen screen door in his Sunday suit and with his hat
held out on the flat of one hand before him like a whole
chicken getting carried to the table on a platter. It was a
kind of roasty brown hat; funny thing, when your mind
said it looked like a roasted chicken in the dark light of the

Bitners' kitchen, you could almost smell roasted chicken over the smell of sour bread there.

"I know him," I said.

"Course ya know him," Mrs. Bitner said. "Course ya know the best lookin man in Saskatchewan; it's where you got parta *your* good looks from, I betcha."

Uncle Emil Beckmann never said anything, so why would I? But I couldn't look like Uncle Emil Beckmann even if I wanted. He was the outside part; he was one of the outside parts. Uncle Emil Beckmann was Gerda's papa, but he was one of the outside parts. Auntie Elizabeth and Gerda and Murray, they were inside; they were Papa's and mine. Uncle Emil Beckmann and even Mama, somehow, they were the outside.

So for a minute nobody said anything. I wished Albertina and I could go; I was still standing there with my hand all gunky.

Then Uncle Emil Beckmann sniffed a little. He had quite a big nose and so he didn't have to sniff very hard for you to hear it. When he sniffed, Mrs. Bitner did too. "Oh-oh," she said. She turned around to Zenina and said, "I guess the darn stuff went and soured on you again."

Zenina stood. The three little boys went around her in a circle and stood too. "Oh well," Mrs. Bitner said, "we can always put a little more jam on it; tastes better that way anyway, don't it, kittens?" And the three little boys all shook their heads up and down hard, yes, yes, yes.

Then Mrs. Bitner and Uncle Emil Beckmann went and sat down at the kitchen table, only first Mrs. Bitner reached down into a floor cupboard and brought out a dark green bottle.

"Last year's cranberry," Mrs. Bitner said.

"I remember," Uncle Emil Beckmann said.

Mrs. Bitner went back to the cupboard and fetched two milk tumblers to the table and poured bright red cranberry wine out of the green bottle.

"Come on," said Albertina. She said it low, I could hardly hear her, I was watching Mrs. Bitner and the bottle and the milk tumblers with the red church velvet wine pouring into them, but Albertina pulled me on the arm and so I knew she'd said, Let's go.

"If you're off to fetch them cows," Mrs. Bitner said, as soon as she saw us going, "forget it; Sabrina's already on her way to the pasture. Why don't you find young Alvena there a pair-a overalls to put on over that nice pretty dress and take this wild buncha kittens here outta Zenina's hair for awhile and go see if you can find down by the ravine, maybe, a few nice strawberries."

"It takes long, unless with the pony cart," Albertina said. "And there's the milking."

"You just never mind the milking," Mrs. Bitner said. "You just have yourself a time with young Alvena there. Mr. Beckmann and me, we'll tend to the milking, now won't we, Floydie?" Mrs. Bitner said, lifting her milk tumbler of red cranberry wine first to him and then to her mouth; it was a funny thing to me to hear Uncle Emil Beckmann get called Floydie.

"It's a part of his name, didn't you know that?" Albertina said. We weren't with the pony cart, we were walking. "It's a part of his name and he likes it better; only nobody ever calls him it and so *she* does."

"I'm going to school next year," one of the little boys said. He was walking backwards in front of me; he was pretty good at it. He watched me all the while; he never seemed to have to look down for rocks or for gopher holes or for anything.

"I'm going too," said one of the other little boys. He was walking beside me. For a while he kept putting his hand into mine, but I kept taking it out again; his hand was gunky and sticky.

"I'm going too," said the littlest little boy. He was walking between me and Albertina. We each had one of his hands. It felt nice. It was warm and smooth and small, almost like a baby's yet, and it had no gunk on it.

"You're *not*!" the other two little boys told him. The one leaned over and yelled it across my stomach at the littlest one walking between me and Albertina, and the other stopped walking ahead of me so he could stick his finger into the littlest one's belly just when he said *not*! We had to stop fast so as not to run over him.

"*Next* year you go," Albertina said to the littlest one. "After the twins go," she said to him. "When the wheat gets nice and yellow the twins go. And then comes the snowtime. You like the snowtime, remember? And then comes the springtime and you bring Zenina crocuses from the pasture, and *then* pretty soon you go. But first you have to stay home and be nice to Zenina; Zenina would cry without you when the twins go. You have to stay home with Zenina a while so that Zenina won't cry."

"You have to stay home with Zenina," said the little boy who had poked him in the belly. He was walking backwards again.

"You have to stay home. With Zenina," said the little boy who was walking beside me. He put his hand in mine again. It was still gunky but I let it stay.

We got to the strawberry patch in the ravine and it was real nice there. There were a quite a few strawberries; Albertina said right away we should have brought more than two jam pails to pick them.

Everybody looked hard and picked hard, even the little boys. Albertina kept telling them to pick nice ones for her because it was her birthday. And every time she said it was her birthday, one of the little boys said, "There's gonna be cake!"

The strawberries they brought to Albertina, whole, she put in her jam pail to take home for supper. But the ones they brought her all squashed and gunked in the hand, she ate out of that very hand, going Num-num-num into it while she ate the strawberry, and making them giggle. But mostly they ate what they picked. When they brought their squished ones to me, I said, "Oh my, that's a nice one," and picked it off their hand with two fingers and then threw it away when they went to find another one to pick.

When we got back to the house the milking had got done and the separating was done, too. And Mrs. Bitner and Uncle Emil Beckmann were sitting at the table again. She had on a clean house dress and he had on a pair of overalls; he didn't even have a shirt on, he had bare skin showing where his shirt should be. It looked funny; I don't think I ever before saw Uncle Emil Beckmann without a Sunday suit on.

The table was set for supper and Zenina and Sabrina were just dishing up. There were no presents on the table, so I didn't think I should get mine from my school bag. I thought maybe Albertina had got her presents in the morning, then. She never said anything about presents all day and somehow there was something in me that wouldn't let me ask.

For the birthday supper we had red sausage. Red sausage is almost always the good kind. Mrs. Bitner said it was Abe Hoffer red sausage and Uncle Emil Beckmann said for sure, he could always tell it, anybody could tell Abe Hoffer's red sausage, Abe put enough pepper in it and he used the bigger guts all the time for the casing because he said it meant less to clean.

I hardly had any. It was all pepper, and on the plate the pieces weren't cut nice, they were just torn off, they looked too much like the men horses when they'd got done letting their water out. My Cousin Abe Schroeder said that once, at somebody's wedding where they had Abe Hoffer red sausage. It made me kind of sick then; I was eating a piece when he said it and somehow my mind wouldn't let me forget.

At our place Papa made the red sausage little. It wasn't so much pepper, either, it was more just meat and smoke.

Mama put it on the table in a nice round ring tied together at the ends for the smoke house, and you cut yourself nice thin little pieces like quarters or like buttons off a winter coat. Or you got Papa to cut it for you, when you were little. And then it was nice.

"It was supposed to be roast pork tonight, except Zenina had to bake bread today," Mrs. Bitner said. "It was supposed to be a nice roast-a pork. You'da liked that, wouldn't you, Floydie; you always liked a nice roast-a pork."

I took a little bite of Abe Hoffer red sausage and I chewed it and told my mind to tell me it was roast pork, nice and brown and with gravy, but somehow it didn't seem to work.

"It was gonna be roast pork," Mrs. Bitner was still saying. "Zenina was all set for it, it's Albertina's birthday, but then she had to bake."

"Well well well," said Uncle Emil. "And how old is this birthday girl?" I looked up. He was smiling with his white, white teeth across the table at Albertina. Albertina had her head down. She seemed to set her mouth, her teeth.

"Eleven," said Mrs. Bitner. "Eleven years old and bigger already than all her sisters, don't they grow up fast though, it takes your breath away. And look at the hands on her, would ya now, Floydie? Don't you see the milker's hands on her? Since she was nine years old, she's been the best dang milker in the bunch."

All inside me, whilst Mrs. Bitner was saying all that, it felt nice and warm and singing, especially around the head. It was like when you'd just got done hearing somebody say something nice about *you*, instead. Albertina put her head up for a little when Mrs. Bitner said the part about the milking, and you saw her draw the mouth in and so you knew she had given her mind the orders not to smile about it and think herself big. Then right away she put her head down again and looked at her plate again and ate red Abe Hoffer sausage in big bites again; I wondered how she could.

"Well well well," Uncle Emil Beckmann said once again, "it seems to me all that deserves something." And he went into an overall pocket and brought out money and gave Albertina a dollar across the table. She wouldn't put out her hand for it but the little boy beside her, he stood up on his chair and reached across for it and took it and put it beside Albertina's plate.

Then Uncle Emil Beckmann went into another overall pocket and came out with some change and picked it over and gave the three little boys each a nickel, and he gave me one too. It seemed a funny thing to me he would have the money in his overalls and not in his Sunday suit.

I took my nickel and I knew it was a kind of present. And now that Uncle Emil Beckmann had given Albertina a dollar for a birthday present I thought maybe I should go to my school bag and get my present for Albertina and give it to her, but you shouldn't really leave a table if supper isn't done.

So I stayed there. "Thank you, Uncle Emil," I said. When I said it out loud, I only said the Uncle Emil part, but in my head I always said Uncle Emil Beckmann every time; it was like my mind wanted me to remember he was not Uncle Emil Schroeder. When Uncle Emil Schroeder smiled, he smiled with more than just his teeth.

And I wondered there, after a little minute, if I should have said, "Thank you Uncle *Floydie*." I tried it inside myself, but somehow the mind wouldn't make the name, it wouldn't get it ready to say, even just inside.

Nobody else said thank you. The little boys' eyes got round and they took their nickels and held them tight in their hands while they ate. We had potatoes boiled in their outsides. So sometimes the little boys had to put their nickels down to cut away at their potatoes; they were still winter potatoes and so the outsides were tough. But mostly they just gave a little pull at the arm of Albertina or Sabrina or Zenina — whichever they were sitting by; each one had a sister to sit by him and help him. And then they would open the hand and look at their nickel while the sister cut their potato or their sausage and then gave them a little poke to tell them it was cut and so it was time for them to eat some more.

Turnips was the other thing for supper. They had lots of butter in them and no pepper, and at the Bitners' — not at our place, Mama wouldn't let you — you passed the sugar bowl and each one put a little sugar nice and even all across the top, and so they were good.

For afterwards, for the dessert part afterwards, there was a cake, flat in the pan, no candles, only Zenina or somebody had printed HAPPY BIRTHDAY SIS in the icing with a knife. Albertina got to cut it.

"You take the first piece, remember," Zenina said. It was the first time anybody but Mrs. Bitner or Uncle Emil Beck-mann had spoke — except for me when I said thank you for my nickel.

But when Albertina cut the first piece, she put it instead on *my* plate. I felt honoured, real honoured. I told Alber-tina later that night in bed I bet it felt to me like it must have felt to Sir Lancelot when King Arthur's queen gave him something nice. Only I didn't tell her I wished I could have had the cake on a clean saucer, and not beside the left-over Abe Hoffer red sausage I couldn't eat on my plate.

We had strawberries, too. Sugared. And with evening's cream on them. We'd got enough strawberries for every-body to have lots, and were they ever good.

It was nice to be in bed with Albertina that night, after I gave her her present, private, and she read the poem and put one of the red bandana hankies in her overall pocket for school next day and put the others in the back of a dresser drawer. Albertina had two dresser drawers to herself, thank Christ, she said, now that Ernestina had got married and was gone.

It was nice, very nice, to lie in bed there, the feather tick kicked off and your bare legs getting the night breeze from the open window in the Bitners' attic.

We talked whispers, mostly. And Zenina and Sabrina talked whispers too, across the room in the other bed.

Once I heard one of them say, "the sonofabitch". She said it pretty mad, even if it was in whispers. I don't know if it was Sabrina or Zenina. Only right away the other one told her to shush.

I woke up once. The dog was barking, and I heard the sound of Uncle Emil Beckmann's car starting up. Or at least somebody's. And I heard it kick a little gravel and start off, and that's all I heard of that. I was petered out. When a party is good, it's good, and then it's awful easy to sleep.

He should of stayed at home already, if he was gonna act so stupid all the time. Even Miss Benedict said so. Otto Uhrich had too big a head; he thought himself smart, even Miss Benedict said so, and he shouldn't of been in school anymore, he was sixteen and bigger already than the School Inspector. So why wasn't he at home already, instead of coming back to school yet every winter and acting so stupid all the time? He was a pain, a real pain, and nobody, not even Miss Benedict could stand him.

Otto Uhrich was horny. Otto Uhrich was maybe my second cousin but he was horny. If he couldn't get near one of the big girls, recesses, to grab a little grab at the queen's crown jewels, Otto Uhrich would go and act horny with one of the guys he could handle.

Big or little, Otto Uhrich could handle just about anybody; he was big as a ox and he had arm muscles like baseballs and he wore tight shirts with the arms rolled up to show his long winter underwear and the big baseball arm muscles.

And when he grabbed, you'd better be quick, or you'd soon know what it was to holler. Even if you were big too,

like John Peters. John Peters was big, but skinny; he was
fifteen but he had no whiskers yet, not even peach fuzz. He
even had a skinny face, a skinny white face with the cheeks
all sunk in like a ghost skeleton and too many teeth though
nice and white. Too white, somehow.

Otto Uhrich was a real pig. If there were no girls handy,
recesses, to get their crown jewels grabbed at, Otto Uhrich
would grab you even if you were a guy, unless you were his
brother, and then he daresn't. He'd grab you and shove
you, your back hard up against the north wall of the coal
shed, and then he'd whump whump whump his big hard
body against yours, his head bent back over his shoulder
grinning Look here at me, grinning like the ginger tom cat
over at Grampa Schroeder's the night he came home and
ate the five new ginger kittens all but the heads.

Whump whump whump, Otto Uhrich would whump his
body against John Peters or Gussie Schroeder or Freddie
Uhrich — the Freddie Uhrich that was his second cousin,
not the one that was his brother; his brother would of told.

So the guys, fourteen, fifteen, some younger even, they'd
get grabbed whenever Otto Uhrich was feeling horny and
they'd get whumped so hard against the north wall of the
coal shed it made me sick to watch it.

How come they didn't come away flat as pancakes, I
don't know, but it made me sick to watch it. It was like the
time Mama had a feather stripping at our place and all the
men came too, along with their wives or girlfriends, to play
blackjack in the parlour and smoke cigarettes and drink little shots of Old Mr. Bill Knopp's homebrew out of milk
tumblers, whilst Mama and the women stripped the prickly
parts out of the duck and goose feathers in the kitchen.

No kids came. No kids came to the feather stripping that
night, only me; I belonged; I was Mama and Papa's and so I
belonged there.

And in the little bit of a party after the feather stripping,
the men and women they joined up sides to have a pull-tag.

No rope. Only arms around the waist, each by each behind each other, no man on the same side as his wife. And then they started to pull, the two lines, man-woman, man-woman, with two men facing in the middle because they had the strongest hands. One was Papa and one was I forget.

And Mama was on the far end of the line; not in Papa's line. She was on the far end by the wall.

And people were squealing. That was mostly the women, except maybe one of the Old Mr. Bill Knopp boys, a bachelor and a high squealer. And people were haw-hawing and breaking out of line to go get another swallow of homebrew out of a milk tumbler so that they could pull harder or to get another one of Mama's doughnuts, big as a tea saucer and sugared all over nice. That was mostly the men. The women didn't drink homebrew, only coffee, lots of it, and they didn't like sugar from doughnuts on their hands to strip feathers or play pull-tag, it was messy.

And so Mama wound up on the far end of one line.

And I was watching. I was licking the sugar off a doughnut and watching. I was small yet, and somebody said out loud later I should of been in bed two hours ago.

I didn't like Mama at the end of the line. The men, and the women too, were big, pretty big, and Mama was a little one always. And so I went and put my doughnut away, the sugar was tasting of tin. Whenever you got a scare in your insides, funny thing, whatever you were eating, even a sugar doughnut, right away it started to taste of tin.

And I was going to go and pull Mama away from all the squealing and the pulling. I ran to her, but right then the other line let go and Mama's line of pullers smashed back into the wall, whump, and Mama screamed; she screamed smashed tight against the wall under Oma and Opa Uhrich's wedding picture, looking down tight-eyed like they sure didn't like it; and how could I know Mama was really only laughing? I threw up my three sugar doughnuts, the ones before the tin one, all over a open bag of feathers, stripped and ready for the pillow tick.

And somebody said, real loud, Why in the world now wasn't the kid in bed two hours ago already?

And that was why I hated even guys to get whumped by Otto Uhrich with their backs hard against the north wall of the coal shed.

Miss Benedict found out. Nobody told her. She just came out to holler a little because it was Otto Uhrich's turn to carry coal in for the heater. Even with big baseball muscles on his arm, Otto Uhrich was so lazy he always pretended he forgot. Every time it was Otto Uhrich's turn, he always pretended he forgot.

So there he was, this time, whumping John Peters up against the coal shed wall. And John Peters always looked like a skinny white ghost skeleton, how could anybody even stand to put theirselves so close to him, arm around close to him, so close to those white teeth? And the other guys, all the other guys, they were standing around, too, grinning and groaning out Umph Umph Umph with every solid whump. And a piece away were standing the big girls, making round cherry mouths over it, and shaking their heads at each other and asking each other if somebody should go in and tell Miss Benedict.

"Miss Myse I would have," Francine Hoffer said. "Miss Myse you could tell anything. But this one? How're you gonna tell a one who can't even do a Nature Science on cross-breeding the milk cow without getting red right up to the ears that Otto Uhrich is as horny as they come and oughda be knifed if he's gonna come back to school every winter until he's thirty."

A joke. Francine Hoffer was a quite a kidder. You didn't have to go to school — nobody could make you — after you were sixteen. But right then I didn't know that yet.

"I wish *I* was thirty," I said. If you were one of the little girls, you weren't supposed to say things when the big girls were talking, but somehow I hardly ever cared; if I wanted to say something I said it. "If *I* was thirty," I said, "I sure wouldn't hang around this stupid old school doing stupid old Arithmetic day after day."

Francine looked at me and her round mouth went straight and her eyes looked right through you.

"Scram, kid," said Francine. Francine was a funny one. She would fuss over you one day and the next day it was like you were dirt to her. "Quit hanging around the coal shed," Francine said, "you might learn something. You beat it on over to the slide hill with the kids your own age before you learn something."

Well, when I didn't want to, nobody could make me. I stood.

"This is a *British* school system and I shall toler-ate *no* foreign tongue ee-ven in the *school* yard." Francine flung her long wool scarf over her shoulder like it was a English wool shawl and began to copycat Miss Benedict. "I *repeat*," Francine said, "this is a *British* school," and then she quit, snap. Francine Hoffer's mouth just closed snap, and she and Emma Schroeder and Helga Uhrich they turned fast and walked away arms around, and Francine Hoffer was in the middle, who else.

And there sure enough came Miss Benedict, her long thin grey wool shawl wound around her long thin self, and the empty coal pail in one hand.

She looked real mad. She looked real mad looks at Francine Hoffer and Emma Schroeder and Helga Uhrich, or at least at their backs. She looked real mad at me too.

"Have you by any chance seen His Honour Mr. Otto Uhrich, Alvena?" she said. The words she said weren't the mad kind, but still she sounded mad when she said them.

I pointed to the north end of the coal shed.

So she went there, stepping with her long legs high high high through the deep soft white new snow, the drag of the coal pail making a porcupine tail trail in the snow beside her.

I went too.

"And just what is the meaning of this?" she said when she got there. And then she had to say it again because Otto Uhrich was still whumping.

"I seem to recall, Mr. Otto Uhrich, sirrah, that you were required today to supply the coal for the school heater," she said, winding the long thin grey wool shawl even tighter around herself and talking so fast she spit little balls of spit out of her mouth in the light of the morning sun.

"If you can interrupt your flagrant hooliganism for a moment or two," Miss Benedict said, "I would appreciate a scuttle of coal delivered to the schoolhouse at once before you return to this pretty enactment from the life of Attila the Hun."

And Otto Uhrich just stood there. Leaned up against John Peters against the north wall of the coal shed, he just stood there, grinning.

"Did you hear me, you thick-witted young Prussian Hun?" Miss Benedict said, loud as the pastor in church when he is promising you Hell. "Let go of your victim immediately and snap yourself onto the end of this coal scuttle; it's nearly freezing again in that hovel you people choose to call a schoolhouse."

Otto Uhrich leaned. John Peters looked white and sick. He sort of sagged there as best he could under Otto Uhrich's big hard body up against the coal shed.

And Miss Benedict just all at once lifted the coal pail and swung it whap at Otto Uhrich's head.

And she hit him.

And Otto Uhrich grabbed for the coal pail and Miss Benedict was still somehow hanging on to it.

And they all went down, him and Miss Benedict and the coal pail and her long thin grey wool shawl, into the soft white snow by the north wall of the coal shed.

And there was a whole lot of rolling around. And for a while Otto Uhrich was on top and for a while Miss Benedict and half her wool shawl were, and for a time or two it seemed to me it was the coal pail.

And then Otto Uhrich was on top, and he had Miss Benedict nailed down, his two big hands grabbing her two skinny ones done up in skinny white leather gloves, no wonder she was freezing. And so there were the both of them laying stretched out there in the soft white snow — only pretty packed down by now from all the rolling — there by the coal shed.

And he was staring bull hate into her, his eyes two hands away from her eyes.

And she never said a word. I went closer. I thought of Mama. Miss Benedict's eyes were wide. Like Mama's when she hit the wall at the party, at the feather-stripping party.

And nobody said a single word.

And then Otto Uhrich raised up his hinder, his knees digging into the snow on either side of Miss Benedict's long skinny legs. And he went, slow as slow against her, whump whump whump.

And then he pushed himself away. And he got up out of the snow and took the coal pail and went into the coal shed and came out with it piled high full of coal.

And nobody said one single solitary word.

And Miss Benedict wormed herself out of the snow by the north wall of the coal shed, and she shook the snow out of her long thin grey wool shawl but she didn't even wind it around herself, she just held it.

Her cheeks were all rosy.

And when Otto Uhrich went by her with the full coal pail, not looking, she stepped through the snow hop, hop, hop, into the big wide long hoofprints of his big manurey old *feld stiefel* and followed behind him up the hill to the school.

And there she jumped ahead of him quick, and held open the porch door for him, and they both went into the porch, the north porch where there was never any sun in winter, and the door shut without a sound right away behind them.

Papa said afterwards that she'd just been gone too long. And Mama said, Oh yes, you would say that, it's on *your* side; there's just all kinds of excuses when it's someone on *your* side. And Papa said, No, it's not that; people change theirselves sometimes, they can't help it; they come back and they've got theirselves all squared away with the world, sort of, and how're you gonna fix a squared peg into a round hole, no shape, no shape whatsoever.

My Aunt Emma was a looker. My Aunt Emma on Papa's side was a looker, a good looker, very good, eyes all asparkle and with white, white teeth, very even; and my Aunt Emma on Mama's side was not, she had nose from both sides of the family and she had no neck. But my Aunt Emma on Papa's side was a very good looker, and everybody who talked about it later said that was half the whole trouble right there: Auntie Emma was a very good looker, and you always had trouble with that kind, everybody knew it.

Eddie Montgomery was a good looker, too, for a man, and tall, not a little shrimp; and he kept his hair cut short even in summer so he didn't get that awful pigskin-white rim where no sun had got at his head when he got barbered for a August funeral or wedding. Most of the men went shaggy bush all summer; Papa too, he said it was cooler; and no matter what the women said, the men got all sunburnt and windburnt all over the face and neck and wouldn't get barbered, and so when they did the white rim just below their hatbands said farmer, farmer, farmer. And in those days the young women in town sure cared, and the young guys who went to the Avenue G Hall to dance, Fridays, all spiffed up and even quoting "The Rime of the Ancient Mariner", some of them, to impress the young city women in their short skirts and bobbed hair — some of them peroxided, even — the young guys got turned down and had to lean against the wall, ankles crossed and with half of a smile out of one corner the mouth, flicking cigarette ashes away with the tip of a little finger, snap, snap, and trying to look casual as anything, but all the same they cared.

Eddie Montgomery was not casual; he was sincere. He would never go to town to dance with the peroxided young women at the Avenue G Hall, he was too proud. And Mama said, Good for Eddie. And Papa said, You too, huh? He's got all you women wrapped round his finger, you wouldn't think to look at him he's a dunce; his old lady's got him wrapped around her finger and he's got the rest of the women wrapped around *his* finger; he's a dunce.

And while he was talking Papa was peeling potatoes for the potato salad for the school picnic supper, so Mama pointed her chin (her hands were busy) at him peeling potatoes and she said, You should talk; let a man walk in the door this minute and you'd hear who is wrapped around a woman's finger, peeling potatoes in the kitchen with the women. And Papa said a man had to defend himself some way, and a potato-peeling man was one who heard a lot when women like my Aunt Emma came to visit. The women talked women talk when they were washing diapers or peeling potatoes, Papa said, Mama needn't think *he* was the one was the dunce: he knew he could learn more about his own sister in one hour listening to her and Mama than he did the whole two days she went fencing with him. All he learned then, Papa said, was she could still set fence and let's see any man outdo her on the wire stretcher.

But that was before. The fencing and the potato peeling was before the school picnic dance when everything blew apart forever. Eddie Montgomery and Aunt Emma making a pair of it was before too, but I don't know all the stuff on that, only everybody said Aunt Emma was a awful lucky woman, considering.

I guess when they said it they were thinking quite a bit about the baby. The one that showed up at my Uncle Rudy and Aunt Bertha's after Aunt Emma left home to go cook in a girls' school in Toronto — who'd ever heard of going so far away from Saskatchewan, only men did that. And my Uncle Rudy and Aunt Bertha went away on a trip to the States, they said, because Aunt Bertha had finally got in the family way, they said, after years and years and years; and they stayed away five months and when they got back they had this baby got born ahead of time, they said. Uncle Rudy had to drive like all get-out, they said, to make the border, to make it a Canadian baby and not a Yankee one. But they told the story a little bit different every time they told it.

And when Aunt Emma came back to visit a few years later when Rudy and Aunt Bertha and little Elizabeth had moved to Chilliwack to take on a fruit farm, she wasn't wild anymore and lots of times her eyes didn't have sparkles in them, they had veils, gossamery veils, like the wings of honey bees or fairies, hard to explain but handy things to have, they stopped people from asking too many questions when you brought those veils down over the sparkle in your eyes.

One thing about Eddie Montgomery: he never asked questions. Papa said it was because he couldn't think of any. And Mama said, Oh you, why don't you get out of here? But Aunt Emma laughed, and came over and kissed him, her own brother; Germans aren't supposed to do that.

And Mama went on to speak on the subject of Eddie Montgomery while she ironed the wash in one corner of the kitchen, using the new gas iron Aunt Emma had brought her from Toronto. It scared her to death, Mama said. What if it explodes? she said. And Aunt Emma said, No different from the gas mantle lamp, are you going to throw it out and go back to candles? But of course Mama wasn't, and it was too hot, summers, to heat the sad irons on the wood stove, so she held her mind tight against explosions and ironed the wash with the new gas iron going sssss-sssss-ss-ss-ss depending on how many frills and fripperies was on the stuff she was ironing.

Eddie Montgomery, Mama said, sss-sss-ss, was a very good and dependable man. He didn't give himself airs for being a Englishman, ssss-ssss-ss, like some of them did, years ago, before the stupid krauts got to buying up all the Hudson Bay pre-emptions, ss-ss-ss, and bidding in high bidder on all the farm sales because they didn't waste their time riding to hounds or holding garden parties when the men should have been out haying and the women baking their own bread. Eddie Montgomery, Mama said, sss-sss-ss, settled right in when his papa went off, back to the old country to be a military man again; Eddie Montgomery ran the place right, even Papa had to admit it, ss-ss-sssss-ss, and he even had a Master Farmer Award, you just tell her how many Germans had *them*, and a woman, ss-ss, would be ss-ss crazy to throw him over again, just to cook in the same girls' school for twenty years and be an old maid in Toronto.

A few more years, Mama said, Aunt Emma would be thirty-seven, the age of Mama, and *then* where would she be, no man in sight?

And Aunt Emma said maybe then she'd be just about ready to start thinking about getting married, and I didn't know before that that people could feel like getting the tingles and wanting to get married at thirty-seven and I said so. And Aunt Emma laughed and said, Oh yes, Pet, and at forty-seven too. And Papa waved the potato peeler in the air and said, Try *sixty*-seven while you're at it! But Mama didn't laugh; she shut off the gas iron and said they just encouraged me and then she'd have the job of straightening me out later, Come on, young madame, children should be seen and not heard from, and if you're figuring to get to any picnic by two o'clock you'd best go fetch the eggs to boil for the potato salad, and so I did, Monday's eggs in the Burns's lard pail so that they would peel clean and good.

And the picnic was good, very good. I won three races, fifteen cents apiece, and my friend Albertina Bitner won six; she ran like a deer, graceful, even in her barn overalls. She ran barefoot and graceful and fleet as a deer; I liked those words, I read them once, the fleet as a deer ones, and then I made a poem for Albertina to tell her she ran like that, but later I forgot it.

And at the picnic Eddie Montgomery picked the firsts in the races, he had a good eye and was dependable; and Teacher picked second; and Aunt Emma picked third, she was Eddie Montgomery's Promised. Only Aunt Emma always said she'd got two runners tied for third; every time, she got two runners tied for third and it cost the Race Money two nickels every time instead of one. But when Eddie Montgomery asked her if she was sure there were two tied for third again, six ties in a row, funny thing, Aunt Emma drew down the veils in her eyes and said did he doubt her eyesight? And Eddie Montgomery said, No no, of course not, he just wanted to make sure the Race Money lasted, and he'd like to wind up with a little money ahead for next year, it was always a good idea. And Aunt Emma said, You tell me if you're running short, Eddie; I'm only too glad to make it up out of my own pocket.

And then the races were over, and Aunt Emma called out

over the megaphone — it was really the morning glory horn off of Papa's His Master's Voice Victrola gramaphone, but people called it the megaphone — for anybody who had not won a prize in the races to please come with her to the booth. And she smiled with those nice even white teeth and with no veils drawn down in her eyes, and she jingled her girls' school money in her little beaded money purse to show nobody should say no. And at the booth you got your pick: ice cream or pop or a chocolate bar, or jaw breakers — any colour — or licorice pipes with the red little candies stuck on the pipe end to make the glow of the fire. Only my friend Albertina and I, we'd won, so we didn't get our pick, but she slipped us a treat anyway later on in the day, and coaxed Albertina to take Fat Emma bars to the little Bitner boys, they hardly had anything unless Albertina won lots of races. She said for Albertina to say to the little boys please accept, they were from a fat lady who liked them because they were so cute. A joke. Aunt Emma was not fat; she was kind of skinny, even; she did not have a lot of curves.

So that was the picnic. And at night everybody went to the picnic dance. Well, not everybody; not the ones who went to the Open Hall Church — it wasn't open at all; if they didn't have you on the roll there, paid up, they didn't let you in, you might be just nosey. But most came, they were nearly all dancing Lutherans anyway, and you weren't supposed to go with boys to dances until you were confirmed and had some sense and enough God in the head to protect you. But until you were confirmed, you could go with families, and if you were too little to leave at home, why, you had to come if your folks did, because there was always fires to think of; and anyway, being young sometimes meant you were still sucking and couldn't last at home without your mother with only a sugar tit even if there was somebody who would stay at home with you and miss the dance or the picnic.

Only, most with sucking ones didn't go to dances. How

could you feed the kid private, for one thing; and you could maybe heat yourself up too much and be up all night paying for your pleasure when the sucking one got the colic. But Elmyra Bitner did.

Elmyra Bitner went everywhere. Nobody kept her home now that her old man was in Prince Albert. And even if he was in Prince Albert and the Mounties would keep him there for a long time — take a lesson and behave yourself if *you* didn't want to go there — she had a sucker yet now and then. Mama said a balloon brought them; she was modern, she didn't believe in the stork or in cabbages to teach young people. And Papa said, Ya, one that didn't work right. And Mama said, Are you gonna get out in the field before noon today, or what? Papa was not one of those buying up lots of Hudson Bay pre-emptions and he said weeds were good on summerfallow so long as you cut their heads off before they seeded, but all the ones who wanted to get Master Farmer, like Eddie Montgomery and Mama, they hated Papa's weeds and said so.

So anyway, we went home from the picnic to milk cows and separate. You didn't eat; you didn't have to. Germans know how to feed you at a school picnic supper and there was lunch again — you might as well say second supper — later at the dance.

And it was a good time, very good. Aunt Emma danced with everybody. Eddie Montgomery didn't like it; you could tell because he tried to look proud about it but when he said Sure, sure, go ahead to the guys who came to ask to dance with my Aunt Emma, Eddie Montgomery looked down and wouldn't look anybody in the eyes. And when Mama came by and sat with him and made a tight mouth and shook her head at Eddie about Aunt Emma dancing and dancing, Eddie said, his voice a little too loud somehow, She's come all the way back home to honour the engagement, Tina, so what's one lousy dance?

And I wondered, none of my business, if he was thinking

about how he'd gone to Toronto two years back to find her. He couldn't get her out of his mind, Mama said, it was just too bad his mother had to be so set against it. But I guess he went to Toronto and found Aunt Emma and she took his ring down there in Toronto and they kept on being engaged for two years. And then his mother got used to it, maybe, and Aunt Emma quit cooking in a girls' school — they were awful sorry, I guess, to lose her cooking — and she came home to be Eddie Montgomery's farm wife.

And could she ever dance! But then, we all could. Young girls in puffed sleeve dresses and Shirley Temple ringlets danced with grampas with big white schnurrbarts and barn boots; mothers fat from too many kids and with big bread loaves jiggling under their crepe second-best dresses danced with fathers with bellies big from too much beer and bara hai and schnitzel and sauerkraut. Young men with too much hair danced with young women who did not have enough of it, according to the old folks and the pastor who did not like the way they bobbed it and marcelled it and spit-curled it and hot iron-waved it — and some, did you ever, even peroxided it, like the girls at the Avenue G Hall in town, and came to the school picnic dance looking like sheaves of ripe yellow wheat. People danced the polka and the waltz and the schottische hard, real hard; if you didn't dance hard with lots of foot stomps and Wha-hoos, you might as well stay home and read the Bible. They danced so hard and swung so hard that one time Freida Ulbricht's pumps went flying right out the open window; they swung so hard that one time Mrs. Old Bill Knopp's bloomers got flung right down around her ankles in the four-hand swing because it was all her own big boys doing the swinging in Birdie in the Cage and they thought she was fooling with them when she hollered, Put me down, you buggers; put me down.

And so everybody danced with Aunt Emma; she was like a gypsy queen to dance with, Papa even said it. And not everybody, but lots, danced with Elmyra Bitner too, the ones who went to the Avenue G Hall and had to look casual there, sometimes, when the town girls turned them down, and the ones who rode over to Elmyra's farm, nights, to talk about the Wheat Pool and the Brotherhood of Man.

And then, sure enough, the newest Bitner sucker started to cry from the top of the teacher's desk where four little swaddled-up ones were sleeping, never mind the guitar and two fiddles. And Elmyra Bitner just finished off the polka, two stomps and a kick, and bowed to her partner like she was the one was the man and so supposed to do that, and she hustled over and picked up the squaller and sat on the edge of the teacher's desk and whipped out a bread loaf and began to suckle him.

And the people roundabouts eased away from it, it wasn't nice. And Eddie Montgomery, I heard him myself, said, It's disgusting, she could at least go in the cloakroom. And Aunt Emma said, Excuse me a minute, will you, Eddie? And she got up and went and sat with Elmyra Bitner, and next thing they were laughing so I went too, so as not to miss something; and while Elmyra Bitner's white bread loaf was jiggling up and down with her laughing at whatever Aunt Emma had said, the little Bitner sucker took his mouth away and looked up at me standing over him and smiled all milky-mouthed and droopy-eyed with content. And I thought then and there for the first time that I'd like to have bread loaves too, and feel a sucker do that and see him get so pink-content and smiley.

And two days after the dance, Aunt Emma went back to cook at the girls' school in Toronto — a phone call long distance, it cost three dollars, was all that it took for her to do that. And when she went she wasn't wearing the thin ring with the pimple diamond in it; Papa called it a pimple diamond, he had no respect. And Mama said Aunt Emma would live to regret it, and Papa said he would help out with the train ticket. And before fall work started, Eddie

Montgomery married my other Aunt Emma — the one who had too much nose and who paid you with German prayers when you filled her wood-box and gathered in her eggs.

And my sparkly Aunt Emma sent me new dancing pumps from Toronto the year I was confirmed, and they fitted me so beautiful I could have died for the pleasure of them; and I bet from that time on, for years and years, there wasn't a once I ever missed a dance.

When my Aunt Emma got married — came home and got married — the war wasn't even over yet.

But we were modern, pretty modern already, by then. People had toilets and running water in the houses, some of them, because they had the power. Girls were going off to town to work, and Ernestina Bitner came home because she got divorced.

People had cars. Some people had new cars, even; how did they get them? Papa couldn't seem to. But maybe he didn't really try. He was funny sometimes; he might have thought he shouldn't try to get one; like as if in wartime that would be more than getting his share.

Papa argued sometimes, even with the pastor, there shouldn't be this war. People were killing each other's cousins like they were crazy people, Papa said, and not even thinking the two countries were mingled blood. Bad enough when people fought the French, Papa said; bad enough when people fought the Spanish, Papa said; but now the people forgot the German kings who sat on the English throne and went and fought their own mingled blood; what was wrong, Papa wanted to know, with just getting rid of one crazy man before the craziness spread.

But the people didn't, and so the war got started; and so Papa did what the farmers were supposed to do in wartime: he raised more and didn't try to hide he'd raised it; and he would go when he took grain to town and give blood out of his arms for the soldiers so that they wouldn't bleed to death.

But Papa didn't like the war and he said so, said so to everybody, said so to the pastor; and always, always, funny thing, Papa's voice got louder and louder when he talked about the war; Papa wasn't much of a one, ever, to make a loud, loud voice.

The pastor shushed Papa, shushed him quick. It was right in our house, right in Mama's front parlour. The pastor sat in the best chair, in Papa's big leather chair with the kind of high wings on it, and Papa sat on the horsehair sofa and he itched, I guess, and his voice got louder and louder when he talked about the war.

Papa hardly ever did that; he hardly ever had to sit on the sofa, and when he did he itched, I guess, and so slid himself around this way and that way so as to scratch the itch away without scratching himself, open, right in front of the pastor. And he slid himself around this way and that way and said in his loud voice the war was stupid if for no other reason than because it was a *war*, man!

He called the pastor man just like that; he called him man like as though he wasn't a pastor, he was just a anybody else. And the pastor didn't even seem to be surprised; his eyes just got small and careful, and he looked quick out of the parlour window — he almost got right up out of Papa's big leather chair and looked quick out the parlour window; the Mounties came sometimes, Sundays, to ask, "And how is everything here then, Mr. Albert Schroeder?"

The pastor knew it, and Papa knew it. And Mama always said, "That's what comes of having a sister whose high-and-mighty man has to keep a whole houseful of socialist tracts." And that was Uncle Emil Beckmann. Not Uncle

Emil Schroeder. Uncle Emil Schroeder did not keep a
houseful of socialist tracts, he had enough trouble with just
one little wife; it was funny people should say that — Auntie was not so little, she was bigger than Uncle Emil.

But Papa never seemed to care. When the Mounties
came, Sundays, Papa never seemed to care; he just told
them come right in and check his mail and look over his
books if that is what they were there for; and if they
couldn't understand the German in his Bible, tell him,
Papa always said for a joke, and he would sure translate.

So you could tell Papa didn't really like it when the
pastor told him, Shush, shush, shush; *God* will decide what
is wrong or right; and if young men got sent to fight for
their country and died, why, the young men would live in
heaven for doing their duty, for doing what they were told;
it would be the old ones who sent them — if it was wrong —
who would fry in eternal hell for it.

The pastor spoke English now. Church was in English
now. Papa spoke what he wanted, English or German. But
it was a funny thing, when the pastor spoke English Papa
spoke German in Mama's front parlour; he wasn't ever a
one to do that; he used to speak always what the other person spoke. But now he was contrary, somehow; it was the
war, maybe, that made him do and be that.

Only, this isn't about the war, and so it shouldn't really
be in here. A person shouldn't put in what doesn't belong,
it only makes a clutter when you are telling things. But it
was, all the same, the war by then, by when my Aunt Emma
came home and got married, and so you have to put that in;
otherwise it's like saying the Jesu was laid in swaddling
clothes in a manger in a barn and not bothering to say it
was in Bethlehem. As it was, Bennie Hoffer figured it happened in Saskatoon somewhere; his ears never bothered to
hear, I guess, the part where it said the Jesu was born in
Bethlehem; and one time, when his folks took him to Saskatoon and it was Christmas, he kept wanting to see Jesu's

barn and hollered like anything when his mama told him,
Now now, don't be so silly.

Bennie Hoffer was always a pretty spoiled one, and when
his mama told Mama that story in our front parlour Bennie
just got up off his knees from the carpet where he was
winding my play train too tight again with the key, and he
stood there in the middle of Mama's nice red gypsy carpet
and hollered, "I bet it says Saskatoon right in the Bible, you
just don't want to read it right!"

And snap, he broke the spring on my play train; it was a
good one and still he broke it; I was maybe six then and
Bennie Hoffer wasn't, even; but he was bigger and more
contrary.

But he doesn't belong in this, either. It's just that the
mind keeps wanting to put lots of things in, sometimes,
when you are telling things; I don't know why it is, only
maybe it wants to get rid of them, somehow, so that it
doesn't have to look at them anymore, and see the pictures
about them anymore, there behind the eyes — or sometimes
in front of the eyes, depending on how much they had plea-
sured you or hurt you.

The pictures: like Bennie Hoffer with his fat fingers like
round pink sausages just starting to fry in the pan, breaking
the spring on your red and silver play train with the white
wavey stripes and having with it somehow always the nice
smell of coal oil just new from town and in a clean new can.

The pictures: like Papa and the pastor making big eyes at
each other — one, scared eyes; and the other, power eyes —
and Mama coming in to the parlour with pound cake and
little wee tiny glasses of apricot brandy and looking Papa,
snap, right in his power eyes and saying, "That's enough
now, Albert!" and shutting him right down like snapping
the key-bolt back into the bar on the windmill when the
horse water trough is full and overflowing again.

The pictures: like Aunt Emma coming home to marry the
American who had no business in the war, but who came

over and joined up in Toronto, anyway, and got to know my Aunt Emma and fell in love of her there before he went overseas and had the war blow off both his legs.

There was *this* thing about my Aunt Emma: if you were in love of her, sincere, she thought she owed you something. Papa said it. There was this other thing about my Aunt Emma: if she loved *you*, you knew it; but if she didn't love you — if she didn't even *like* you — you could go a long, long time and never even know.

It was Papa's way, too, in a way, maybe: but I don't know for sure. More likely Papa was a one who didn't know how *not* to love or like.

I don't know about the American. I didn't know him from before the war; he wasn't around then, before the war shot off both his legs. But for a while there, after Aunt Emma brought him home to the farm to our house — they came in a airplane, a airforce airplane and everything; they came to Saskatoon but I couldn't go along with Papa to fetch them, Mama wouldn't let me — for a while there when Aunt Emma brought the American home to our house, to the farm to our house, in a wheelchair and everything and then never left him alone for a minute I thought maybe Mama was right. For a while there, after Aunt Emma married the American in the church where the pastor made even some of the old men cry by talking about sacrifice, I thought maybe Mama was right when she told Papa, private, in the kitchen, "Your sister would of been twenty times better off with Eddie Montgomery, but she's a real Schroeder of course, and the Schroeders, it seems, seem to have trouble finding somebody good enough for them — and *now* look!"

"Well, I don't know so much about that," Papa said, "I found *you*, didn't I?"

"Well, just look at them out there," Mama said. "See the way he fidgets? I bet you he's telling her he don't like the way she's got his shawl folded. I bet you he's telling her he don't like the weight of the apple blossoms falling on his lap. Look, look," Mama said, moving out of the way and making room for him at the window, "what did I tell you? There she is fussing, brushing something off his lap. Oh, I just don't know," Mama said, "some men would be by now at least trying the crutches, but he — he won't even so much as try."

"He's a injured man," Papa said. "A person has to remember, he's a injured man." Papa didn't come to the window though Mama stood there holding back the window curtains for him. "He took a awful wallop to the body, sure, but who's to tell how hard it hurt him in the mind."

"You mark my words," Mama said, "he'll run her a dance to the end of his days; the Schroeders seem somehow always to need that."

And maybe Eddie Montgomery thought so too, I don't know. He didn't go to the war or anything, Eddie didn't. He stayed home and farmed and flew the Union Jack from a flagpole in his mama's garden, and he talked about his *pater* who went years ago to war before there was even a war to go to.

It looked real nice, really nice, the way the Union Jack flew in Mrs. Montgomery's garden. She had no rows or anything in the garden. It could be Mrs. Montgomery didn't understand about rows, maybe. She called it her English garden and for years, when I was little, I thought that that meant weeds.

Anyway, Eddie Montgomery got married right away, years ago, when my Aunt Emma came home once from Toronto with Eddie Montgomery's engagement ring on her finger and then went back to Toronto again almost right away, leaving Eddie Montgomery his little pimple diamond ring.

When she did that, Eddie Montgomery took that little pimple diamond and gave it to my other Aunt Emma, the one on Mama's side, and married her as quick as anything, as if he was saying, So there then! So there!

And after my Aunt Emma came back home and married the American in our church with the pastor saying everything in English, talking in English about giving your life and your limbs to a holy, blessed cause, why, Eddie Montgomery never seemed to bring my other Aunt Emma along whenever he came around to talk.

"Well, and what's Sister up to today?" Mama would say, Mama said one day when he came back again. "She's too busy to stop around for a minute one of these days and talk?"

"Oh, she's *ennsy-ahnt* again," Eddie said. "You know how it is, Tina; it's considerably better for junior-to-be not to travel; and more than that, Emmy says a man with no knees simply makes her feel quite, quite upset."

Eddie Montgomery had this funny way of talking, always. Sometimes it seemed to you he had learned his talking from straight out of a book.

"She could sit here in the kitchen with me," Mama said. "I hardly ever see the use, nowadays, of my own front parlour, for I don't seem to take a man, no knees, too good these days myself."

And all the while that Eddie and Mama talked, Eddie kept looking towards the parlour. But as soon as he got up from the table where Mama was giving him coffee she said to him, "You know you don't have to go on into the parlour and help entertain them, Eddie. You been too good already, coming around so often. You could just stay here with me in the kitchen and visit."

But Eddie didn't sit down again, he set his chair back into its place around Mama's kitchen table. That was one thing Mama liked about Eddie Montgomery: *his* mama had trained him to put the chairs back into their places at the table when a person was done eating; a few other people, Mama sometimes told Papa and me, could take a few lessons from Eddie Montgomery before they walked out of Mama's kitchen again not thinking.

Eddie Montgomery stood there behind his chair at Mama's kitchen table and with his two hands sort of real tight on the chair back, not saying anything, just looking every other minute towards the parlour door.

"Those that make their beds ... you know, Eddie," Mama said. "She had to have her way, and now she's got it: complaints, complaints, complaints; I never heard the like of it in all my life. He's too hot or he's too cold or the shawl over his lap itches. Itches his *feet*, can you imagine it! That's what he says itches: his *feet*. Let me tell you, it gets to a person; I'll be glad when they go back to Toronto. There's more to that whole business than meets the eye, Eddie, let me tell you that."

"Well," said Eddie. He said again, "Well." Then he turned without saying anything more and went off into the parlour to sit and watch for Aunt Emma to come and get run a dance by the American with no legs; to sit and watch her fuss over the American's shawl and his hair and his chair and his pillow; to sit and watch her with something sorry lying there at the back of his eyes.

And when I saw him watching her like that, and when I heard the American say one more time, "For Christ sake, not like *that!*" to my Aunt Emma, I sometimes wished she hadn't got so contrary about Eddie Montgomery being so stingy with the nickels for the race money at the school picnic years ago; I somehow wished my Aunt Emma was not hanging like a worry wart over a complaining man in my mama's front parlour, but was somewhere else, and young again, and dancing the one-step at some fast school picnic dance.

And I would go to her then; go to her though it meant I had to go past the American with no knees being all scowls and contrary in the wheel chair. I would stand there beside her until she stopped, for a minute, doing fluttery things for him. "Hello, sweet pet," she would say then, taking my hand for a minute and laying it up to her cheek.

But she would soon put it down again, for the American would be saying his feet itched again. I never could understand him saying that, then; I just thought he was a liar, and contrary. But Aunt Emma let go my hand right away, those times, and said to Eddie Montgomery sitting still and watching across the room, "You'll have to forgive us, Eddie. I think Hugh wants to go to his room now; he's a bit tired, I think."

And Eddie would jump right up and say, "Anything I can do? Anything at all I can do?" And Aunt Emma would say, "Thank you, no, Eddie. It's been very good of you to call. Very neighborly of you. You'll give my regards to Emma, now won't you?"

"Oh yes, by all means, by all means," Eddie would say, would keep saying like he hadn't said it already. "She's *ennsy-ahnt* again, did I tell you? She's keeping very well in spite of the fact that she's *ennsy-ahnt* again."

"How nice," Aunt Emma would say, and she'd start to push the American to the door and Eddie would sort of gallop across the floor and try to help. And just about then Papa would be coming into the parlour from finishing the chores and he'd try to help from his end. And he'd be saying, "Them old feet again, is it, Hughie-boy? That's tough. That's a tough one, Hughie, but you just hang in there and it will all turn out all right."

And they'd all sort of get jumbled together in each other's way in the doorway. And then they'd all get sorted out again, with Papa and Aunt Emma and the American going down the hall, Aunt Emma saying to Papa, "No, no, Albert; it's all right, I'll do it," whenever Papa reached over and tried to help push the chair.

And Eddie Montgomery would kind of stand there, first on one foot and then on the other. Or he and I would sit and look at each other, and then look away from each other. Eddie Montgomery wasn't a one to talk much to you unless you were grown; if you weren't it was like you weren't there, somehow, to Eddie Montgomery.

And sometimes Papa would come back first from having lifted the American into bed, and doing things with the stumps of his legs so that his mind quit remembering there should be feet there, somewhere at the end of them.

And Eddie would still be there in the parlour. And sometimes it would be Mama who came in first; and she'd say, "Emma just phoned, Eddie. She just phoned to say hello to me; she never asked if you were gonna come home soon, or anything; she just really phoned for no other reason only to say hello to me."

And Eddie would look at Mama sort of as if he hadn't quite heard what it was she said.

"She just did happen to ask if I thought she should maybe put the coffee on for you, but I told her to just take herself right off to bed; that I'd soon have you off home all coffeed and fed; so come into the kitchen, why don't you now; no use to wait for the other two, they might be half the night, and here's a nice berry kuchen just out of the oven; it's a shame for nobody to eat it hot."

Then she'd see me hanging around the corner and she'd say, "And as for you, Miss Mary Contrary, if you want a glass of milk and some kuchen before you go to bed you'd better be real quick about it." And she'd reach for my hinder to give me a good slap there to start me out.

"You should of been in bed hours ago," she'd say. "You have to watch them like a hawk, Eddie," she'd say. "It's as though they don't know what a clock's for, the older they get. Girls are hard to raise; they're so into themselves and contrary; you'd better hope you get another boy."

And in the kitchen she would sit with him and make him take more and more coffee and kuchen, and she'd talk to him and forget about me again until we heard Papa and Aunt Emma coming back down the hall; coming to the kitchen for coffee, too, maybe.

Then she'd sort of quick get up and get Eddie Montgomery up and out the door before Papa and Aunt Emma came into the kitchen.

And she'd say to me, "Don't you understand the king's English? Didn't I say Bed to you twenty times tonight?" And she'd swat-tap me ahead of her, only saying to Papa, "Coffee's still hot; kuchen isn't," when we passed him and Aunt Emma in the hall, and not really saying anything at all to Aunt Emma.

And Aunt Emma would be looking over her shoulder still, toward the room where the American was bedded down for the night. She would have that not-here look in her eyes if she turned to you as you went by. She had a tight and a listening look to her, and it hurt me; it hurt me to see that.

"He'll sleep awhile. Come have coffee," Papa would say. And he would take Aunt Emma by the arm with one hand, and sort of swat-tap her on *her* hinder with the other, along the hall towards the kitchen whilst Mama got me steered around again and did the same to me the other way and up the stairs to my room.

But she never seemed to get me far enough, fast enough, because always, always, I heard my Aunt Emma in the kitchen and starting again to cry.

When Uncle Emil Beckmann moved Gerda and Auntie Elizabeth and the new little boys to town, it hurt me. I never said it, but it hurt me. Hurt me lots and lots.

He moved them to town because Grampa Schroeder said to do it. He bought them the house, secret, private, only he told Papa. Told Papa his little Elizabeth had by The Holies suffered enough. And Papa was a careful man, he never told things, only if you were sitting quiet in his big chair with the high back in the parlour, people sometimes didn't know it when they came in and talked, or else they thought you had no ears, no ears to understand them.

Papa was a careful man and never told things. Mama got too excited. I learned it early. But Gerda was a teller, sometimes; only sometimes. My Cousin Gerda was mostly a listener. When people came she listened too, washing dishes hard, hard, her eyes only on the dishes — she told me once how to do it — or folding towels and sheets, later, in her Mama's new bedroom off the kitchen in town, Gerda listened and sometimes told things.

She had to be sore when she did. She had to be so sore, most likely at Uncle Emil, and then she told things. Otherwise Gerda hardly ever talked.

But before Uncle Emil moved them all to town and it hurt me, Gerda would walk over to our place sometimes, Sunday afternoons. And she most likely would have that lightning in her eyes, that lightning that made her eyes like pale slough ice — Uncle Emil eyes. But she always hung her head quick if it was Mama opened the door to her; I guess it was a danger if somebody like Mama saw the lightning in her eyes. So she always hung her head quick if it was Mama opened the door to her and said, real quiet to Mama, "Mother said I could come play with Alvena a while, so long as it's all right with you."

"She's always hanging her head like that, like a whipped dog," Mama said to Papa this day. "Hanging her head like a whipped dog, like she was the cause of it all. Why doesn't your sister leave that man if she can't get along with him; a lot of women would like the chance to get along with him, but my, she thinks she's so modern, won't go to church, just like your father, she's too good for God, I guess, just like your father, no wonder Emil Beckmann gets ornery now and then, so why doesn't she just leave him, she's modern enough to do it, and your father will give *her* money for a house in town even though *we*, my goodness, can't get the loan of a few dollars for three new milk cows, my goodness, why doesn't she just leave him and go live in town with your father, he always favoured her, you know, you're just too blind to see it, and she can stop looking so long-necked skinny and put-upon all the time and that young Gerda wouldn't have to come around here looking like a whipped dog all the time, it isn't healthy, it affects others, you know, not to mention any names," Mama said, "it hurts others."

When Mama got going, she talked; she never quit. If you tried to say anything, even like, "But Mama, I never broke the pitcher, honest," she just put her voice up another squeaky holler louder and went right on, and if Papa came in, she right away cried a little.

Papa was a quieter one, and he hardly ever interrupted.

But now he said, "Well now Tina, it seems to me there's likely lots of things affects girls Alvena's age. Twelve years or not, it seems to me there's better things for her to do than sit in the house on a nice summer day with her nose in a book. No sunshine likely affects people too, seems to me; she should be out there."

"It's Sunday, leave her alone," Mama said, "she has her good church clothes on; there's more to life than running around outside like a tomboy, riding horses bareback and pretending at cowboys like all the Schroeders. Besides, she's at that stage, you know; she's already had the back pains some, and it could be any time now."

"Oh," Papa said, and got a little bit red behind the beard, and stuffed his hands in the pockets where he stood and chewed on the end of one side of his moustache where it drooped and always got wet in his coffee if Mama didn't warn him first to lift it.

"Well," he said, "I wonder what's the use to talk all the time about things. Things are what they are and we got them cows anyway, remember? A man who has got to go beg from his father is no man. I always said I'd squeeze the money for the cows if you wanted them, so what was the use, really, of mentioning it to him, it might have been better not to do it."

"Oh sure," Mama said, "blame me! I was only trying to help, you know. It's not I take pleasure squeezing tits on three more cows."

"I know, I know, I know," Papa said quick. And he took one hand out of a pocket and held it, sort of, out to her, but a little like he knew she wouldn't take it. "So come on," he said, "how about it? How about at least *you* come out and ride a little horseback like the crazy Schroeders and we'll go check the crop for wild oats; it's quite a while since we did that together."

"Hmph," said Mama, standing a little straighter, like a

queen, but letting her mouth be glad just a little to be asked. "You're a goof sometimes," she said, "and it would be more like checking the crop for crop. If it doesn't rain pretty soon there'll be no green oats even to feed the cows we had, and here's us with three new ones giving milk like rain and eating oat chop by the gallon."

"You worry too much," Papa said. "Come on now, put on some overalls, why not, and come show me how the Uhriches used to play a little cowboy too."

Mama smiled a little when he said that, even smiled wide enough to show the teeth nice, even though she pressed her mouth together quick to shut out the smile. "It's Sunday," she said.

"God don't stop the wild oats because it's Sunday," Papa said. "We could handpick a few down there by the north slough where the wild mint grows. Surprising," Papa said, "how handpicking helps to small up that patch of wild oats."

"Well, I don't know," Mama said, looking at me.

"She's twelve," Papa said. "Nearly a woman. Or are you afraid somebody's gonna come steal her if you go away one little hour?"

And he went out to the porch himself and brought in Mama's little outside chore overalls and held them out to her. And Mama put them on over her dress saying, "Now Alvena, if Gerda comes, you stay in the house and play the organ, only hymns, mind you; or play the little blue *Gospel Songs* book, there's nice ones in there, they're safe." And she gave a little yank to the overalls' braces and Papa stepped over quick to help. "And if I have to say it myself," she said, looking up at him and letting the smile come wide, "I could always rope a calf better than Elizabeth Schroeder or even Abe Schroeder." And she bent and rolled up the pants cuffs three sharp turns apiece. "And if you get back pains again," she said to the pants cuffs, "make a hot water bottle and send Gerda home, she's a little too young yet; and go to bed and stay there and read *Marjorie May's Twelfth Birthday* again, it will help. Papa and I won't be long, only maybe a little hour is all."

"She's OK," Papa said. "She has good sense, just like all the Schroeders." And Mama opened her mouth to be a little sore about that, but Papa gave her a swat on her little overalled hinder and said, "How about them wild oats, then?" And the swat got her going out the door and then she started talking and I couldn't hear what but I heard "roped Papa's bull once" and then there was laughing, Papa's was no surprise but Mama's was, even if it wouldn't of been Sunday.

And I guess I didn't really think it was fair, in a way, not getting asked to go pick wild oats — for a long time *I* was the one had got to go with Papa. Anyway, just all at once the *Ulysses* seemed dull, dull, dull; they'd got old Helen of Troy in there again and it all seemed so stupid, all that killing and for only one woman, who maybe even had a prissy little mouth like Mama — it sure looked like it in the picture.

And so I got up out of Papa's big chair, and the crotcheted chair back slipped off and I didn't even care if Mama came home and saw it, I just left it. And I picked up the little blue book of *Gospel Songs* and all at once I kind of hated even Jesu. And I went out and had a slice of saskatoon berry kuchen; Mama made it good no matter what she put inside it, except she'd got stingy with the sugar again and it didn't taste right, so I left it.

And my back and legs felt draggy, felt like somebody else's, and I went back to Papa's big chair and sat in it, it was still warm from me, and I pulled my feet up under. And there was something caught in the chair back, I thought it was the crocheted chair back and I thought, Darn Mama's darn old doilies! But it was *Marjorie May's Twelfth Birthday* stuck there instead, and I hauled it out and turned the pages again, it was dull, dull, dull; after the first page of it you could tell it wasn't about anybody's birthday, it was a trick to teach you something. I got tired of learning, school was plenty, and so I threw it, but it was so puny little it only fluttered a little ways and then flopped down in the middle of Mama's all-colour parlour rug, its plain blue with a simpy Marjorie May on the cover lying there saying, And what's Mama gonna say when she sees it when she comes?

And then, sure enough, Gerda came. And she had on her Sunday dress, too; not fancy, never anything fancy — Auntie Elizabeth didn't believe in it, and it was only Sundays or to concerts Gerda ever wore a dress, any kind at all. Gerda didn't like dresses, but I did.

To dress up in a clean new dress — or even one still hot from the iron because Mama had washed it out special for the school picnic when you'd got berry pie on it — to dress nice was to feel like a princess, or a queen, only not Helen of Troy. To be a real queen you had to do good things for the ordinary people and give God all the credit besides, not go have somebody make a war because he thought you were too beautiful to be a queen to anybody else but him.

And Gerda even wore a pinafore over her dress, not very nice but a good idea all the same. Gerda had real sweaty hands and she was always wiping them. You try wiping sweaty hands in summer down the sides of your Sunday dress all day and see what your mother tells you come washday.

And Gerda came in and threw her hat on the kitchen table. She swirled it onto the kitchen table like Uncle Abe did his cowboy hat when he came in to wash and eat when he and Papa were cutting pigs or something. Gerda's hat used to be Grampa Schroeder's Sunday one, and she liked it a whole lot. And she said, real quiet, but with those sloughice eyes flashing lightning sparks, "It's so goddam bastardly hot, it's gonna burn all the crops again, and then there'll be some fun."

And I knew Uncle Emil Beckmann was off again to ride his big white stallion over at Elmyra Bitner's. When Gerda came and swore right away, swore a lot all day, before the day was done you'd hear Uncle Emil was off again to ride his big white stallion over at Elmyra Bitner's.

"Mama and Papa went to pick wild oats," I said.

"I saw," said Gerda.

My legs were so darn draggy.

"Wanna play organ?" I said. I wanted to sit.

"Nah," Gerda said. She went ahead of me into the parlour and flopped on the all-colour rug there and so did I.

"What's this?" Gerda said. She'd flopped on simpy old *Marjorie May*. She hauled it out. "Sonofabitch," she said, "I bent it all to hell. I didn't mean to. It's a book." Gerda had this real respect for books.

"It's no book," I said. "It's one of those tricks to teach you stuff, like Uncle Emil's *Brotherhood of Man* books he keeps in his bottom dresser drawer."

"Hmm," said Gerda. And she thumbed it through and pressed it back together, flat, flat, flat. "It's just about rags," she said.

"What kind of rags?" I said. I didn't remember anything about rags in there, I guess I hadn't read in it far enough. I didn't really care, though. I asked but I didn't really care. I lay flat on my back on the parlour rug. My legs were somebody else's.

"*No* kind," said Gerda. "It's just a something that happens. Blood and stuff. So girls can have babies. Mother said."

I sat up. "*I* don't want to have babies," I said. "*I* don't want to have blood. What does the blood do? When do the babies come? Babies come out of the hinder, like calves and kittens. I don't want any dull old babies coming out of *my* hinder," I said, and I felt myself getting sorer and sorer about it. And there were Papa and Mama gone off on horseback to pick wild oats in the sun.

"I don't know and I don't care," said Gerda. "*I'm* never gonna have it. Wanna go out?"

"Mama said not," I said. And then I thought of Mama off on horseback with Papa and how she'd said about roping her papa's bull. So Mama roped calves when she was a Uhrich still, and now I wasn't supposed to, I was supposed to rope only a fence post or sometimes, sneak, sneak, one of the dull old milk cows in the pasture. So I said to Gerda, "Can you rope a calf?"

"Can God spit?" said Gerda, jumping up.

"Don't be stupid," I said. "And don't take God's name in vain, either; you're gonna get caught out one of these times and once the pastor hears I bet you ten cents you go to hell."

"*He* can go to hell," Gerda said. "Pastor and Papa and God can all go to hell, for all of me; see if I give so much as a sonofabitch about it."

When Gerda was that way, what was the use of talking? "Can you rope a calf?" I said again.

"Got a rope?" Gerda said.

So I got up too, and we went out into the sun. It was hot, hot as hell, after the dark coolness of Mama's parlour. So I went back for my sun hat, it was pretty, I liked it, but Gerda seemed to look pretty nice with just Grampa Schroeder's old Sunday hat on her head. And then we walked to the barn and I put my arm around Gerda. She never put her arm around, not on anybody, and she carried herself stiff all the time that *you* did it. But all the same, when you were telling her hard something from the *Ulysses* and so forgot somehow to put an arm around her while walking out to the pasture or the north mint slough or something, she would pick up your arm and put it around herself and walk stiff close beside you, listening.

But this day we went out to the calf corral, not the pasture. And from the lean-to by the chop bin, we got some rope; it was new, almost, full of oily binder-twine smell and smooth and sweat-shiny yet.

And the calves came prancing up to watch us. They came stiff-legged and hopgoblin prancy to watch us. And one stuck his cold wet pink slobby nose up against my bare leg and behind me. And I yelled, "Hey," surprised as anything, and spun around and grabbed him, grabbed him around the neck, so hard he made a aw-w-gh from deep down in the throat where I was hard-squeezing him. And we sort of wrestled, he and I, and Gerda laughed and laughed, and hollered, "Hang on to the little bugger, and I'll rope you both!"

And the calf and I went down then, down together on the hot dirt and straw and you-know-what-maybe-else of the calf corral. And the calf aw-w-gh ed again and thrashed and I was under him but I somehow hung on to his neck, wanting him to say aw-w-gh even harder. And Gerda hollered, full of giggles, "You're buggin' his eyes, Alvena; that'sa way! Here comes the rope!"

And it whanged and was there. And the calf was yanked off me; it was like something had got stolen from me somehow, and I felt a warm warmness worm-crawling slow slow down between my legs. And I got up and lifted my dress, my Sunday dress. And there was the blood.

And the pain was a hurt that went all through me; there wasn't a part of me, not even the part that always used to stand there outside me and never felt things but only watched them, even that part of me felt pain, and knew it, and *was* it, somehow.

And the calf was gurgling aw-w-gh! deep and low and terrible; terrible loud and hard inside his throat. Gerda had the rope around his neck and snubbed around a fence post. The calf was up and had set his clean little growing feet fierce as fierce into the hot dirt of the calf corral and was putting his everything into pulling his own head off.

"Let him go," I said to Gerda. I never knew before that pain had a colour. Now I knew it was all-colour, just like

Mama's parlour rug.

"Won't," said Gerda.

"Let him go," I said, "or I'll kill you where you stand."
And Gerda looked at me, and it seemed her eyes lost their
lightning for a minute, a whole acre and a year of a minute,
while we stood and looked at each other through the all-colour pain of the calf's aw-w-gh.

And then she let him go. And he ran, ran, ran, head-wob-
bling away from us to the far end of the calf corral where he
stood and looked at us, still shaking his head.

It was a hot day but now I was shivery. I lifted my dress
again and showed Gerda the blood.

"It's the rags," she said. "You have to go in the house
and wash up good, Mother said, and tear up an old sheet,
make sure it's an old one, and stuff yourself there, she
didn't really say how, and lie down." And Gerda put her
arm around me and we went to the house and she helped
me do all that.

She didn't know about the hot water bottle, but I remembered it all of a sudden, out of the pain that stood outside of
me and was good at remembering. And so Gerda lit the
stove and got the water so boiling hot in a big flat pan for
the hot water bottle, she had to wrap it in a piece of old
sheet to lay it on my belly; and there was hardly enough hot
water bottle for all the pain.

And Mama said afterwards, "My goodness, didn't the
girl know enough to light the coal oil stove instead to get
hot water in this heat? She's made it like an oven in this kitchen. To light a wood stove in this heat, it makes you wonder," Mama said afterwards, "where the famous Schroeder
brains have got to in that Gerda."

But before Mama and Papa came Gerda kept saying,
"Did it quit yet? Do you hurt yet? Why don't you look at
yourself and see if it's nearly done!" And I told her I hurt
too much. I could still see the calf trying to pull his head
off. I could see him there, about three feet in front of my

eyes, while I lay there on the kitchen couch and was glad it was so warm in there.

"Oh Gerda," I said, "it hurts too much to look at it."

Then Gerda's eyes got the lightning in them again and she said, "Well it's never gonna happen to *me*!" And just then we heard Mama and Papa ride jangling and laughing into the yard. "It's never bloody sonofabitchen hell ever gonna happen to *me*!" said Gerda. And she grabbed her Grampa Schroeder's old Sunday hat and clapped it on her head and slammed the door and was gone.

"She had her head hanging down like a whipped dog again," Mama said as soon as she stepped in the door. "Just like a whipped dog again. Now whatever in the world happened between you and your Cousin Gerda here today?"

"Nothing," I said. "Just nothing," I said. And I turned my face to the wall so that she couldn't see me crying: crying for Gerda, and me, and the blood, and the calves; crying for the way things used to be when Gerda came over and Mama was outside for a while and we sneaked the key to the organ and played *There Was an Old Man and He Had an Old Sow* even though it was Sunday, and laughed so hard we nearly killed ourselves, and switched to *Komm Jesu Schön* the minute Mama came in, and laughed again, later, when she was gone, because she told us we were good little girls to sing so nice on Sundays.

Once upon a time, my Cousin Gerda and I, we had sure had a lot, a lot, of laughs, I told the crying part of me; and I held myself steady so that Mama, if she was watching, wouldn't see and know how I was crying all through me now that Gerda was gone.

209